Mark Mills Pomeroy

Gold-Dust for the Beautifying of Lives and Homes

Mark Mills Pomeroy

Gold-Dust for the Beautifying of Lives and Homes

ISBN/EAN: 9783337418021

Printed in Europe, USA, Canada, Australia, Japan

Cover: Foto ©Andreas Hilbeck / pixelio.de

More available books at **www.hansebooks.com**

POPULAR BOOKS

BY

"BRICK POMEROY."

I. — SENSE.

II. — NONSENSE.

III. — SATURDAY NIGHTS.

IV. — GOLD-DUST.

V. — BRICK DUST.

"The versatility of genius exhibited by this author has won for him a world-wide reputation as a facetious and a strong writer. One moment replete with the most touching pathos, and the next full of fun, frolic, and sarcasm."

All published uniform with this volume, at $1.50, and sent by mail, *free of postage*, on receipt of price,

BY

G. W. CARLETON & CO., Publishers,
New York.

" Please, sir, buy a bouquet for your buttonhole ? "—*See page* 25.

GOLD-DUST:

FOR THE

BEAUTIFYING OF LIVES AND HOMES.

BY

M. M. POMEROY,

["BRICK" POMEROY,]

AUTHOR OF "SENSE," "NONSENSE," "SATURDAY NIGHTS,"
"BRICK-DUST," ETC.

NEW YORK:

G. W. CARLETON & CO., Publishers.

LONDON: S. LOW, SON & CO.

MDCCCLXXI.

Dedication.

To THOSE who are struggling to rise in the world — to those who have hours of sadness, and whose hearts at times are grief-laden — to those who would be happy and who would add to the happiness of others — to those who love each other, and who can say it is good to live for the good we can do through

OUR FRIENDSHIP,

THIS VOLUME of good intent is earnestly and respectfully dedicated by   THE AUTHOR.

CONTENTS.

Chapter	Page
I.—What an Artist does	13
II.—Wanted to Go Back to God	25
III.—Only Thinking	36
IV.—What will We do Over There?	48
V.—A Life Lost	58
VI.—To a poor Little Boy	72
VII.—The Beauty of Life	82
VIII.—Only a Widow	90
IX.—Patient in Suffering	98
X.—Why She Died	111
XI.—The Beauty of Better Work	122
XII.—The Light on the Shore	129
XIII.—Back to her Home	140
XIV.—Dying as We Write	151
XV.—Home, and Why it is Home	162
XVI.—Working and Waiting	170
XVII.—Trying to be Rich	178
XVIII.—Indeed a Golden Reward	189
XIX.—Merely Opening a Door	199
XX.—New-Year Presents for Little Ones	208
XXI.—About a Bright-eyed Baby	217
XXII.—Thinking of the Past and the Future	228
XXIII.—Not so Lonely after all	238
XXIV.—Put them Away	249
XXV.—How some Poor People are very Rich	256
XXVI.—The Loved and the Absent	267

PREFACE.

Twenty years ago!

Almost broken-hearted, — bleeding from excessive punish-ment, a poverty-clutched boy lay under a fence near the road-side. The hot summer sun beat down upon the lacer-ated back of the youth as he slept, overcome with pain, sor-row, despair, and dread of the future. When he crept away to this hiding-place, to weep and suffer — to wonder why he too, could not have friends — to think of a mother in heaven, and to wish he might find with her a home and rest Over There, the future seemed dark, dismal, and treacherous, without one ray of light to guide through the wilderness sep-arating the shores of birth and death.

The poor boy dreamed. A sweet, peaceful dream. The sun sank slowly behind the hills; the evening breeze came with cooling breath, and there, resting on the growing grass, with head pillowed on one arm, this was his vision.

The dark clouds seemed to roll away, leaving a golden reach of atmosphere far extending toward a distant city in the Heavens. From the crowd which seemed to hover over this city there came one with golden hair, radiant face, and look of love, seeming to float as if by the power of the will toward where slept the bleeding sufferer.

Gently to his side she came — sweet kisses on his aching brow impressed — with love-light soothing hand, the tears she wiped from his eyes, and then whispered such words of love and hope that memory holds them ever as sacred keys to Eternal joys.

These were her words : —

"Over There is rest! Be patient, and suffer if need be while here, but trust in me. I went but to prepare for your coming. Do not fear or faint. I will watch over, protect, and guide your feet safely amidst dangers, you little can imagine, even with the vision of dreams. Look upward. Look Over There, where suffering and anguish are unknown. Trust in me; have faith and I will ever come when you are in danger or trouble. Fear not. I never will be long away. The clouds may gather black and thick between us, but I will come on wings of light, never leaving you long alone, as I used to come to the cradle wherein you slept, but not in pain as now."

Then she went away, and the poor boy with a sigh stretched out his hands, but she had gone. Then came a friend, walking by chance that way. With words of cheer, touch of sympathy, and tender care, our wounds were dressed, and kindly sentences listened to. Thus spake that friend : —

"Never mind for the past, its smarts and bruises. The future is as bright to-day as ever! Take courage. Be brave. Never despair, but with earnest endeavor live for the good of to-day and the joys of to-morrow. As others have been cruel to you, be not so to them. It is noble to forgive, and thus comes strength. Do not thank me, but help others when they are in trouble, and life will have more joys for you with each coming year. Do not thank me, but help others as you have been helped."

The poor boy arose to walk in a new light. Kind words lifted him to renewed life. The good seed sown by the way-side took root. Our friend who thus spake has passed away, but oft, and oft, and oft the gentle spirit who came with such sweet gifts to flavor our dreams has smiled on us a thousand times since, as she ever does when we stop to talk with those who are to be found by the roadside, suffering, discouraged, but needing only kind words from a loving heart to waken them to new life and that courage which enables those who strive aright to walk toward the Eternal Gardens bearing their sheaves with them.

God give us all strength to help others — and this is our work.   M. M. P.

Gold Dust.

—oo°°oo—

CHAPTER I.

WHAT AN ARTIST DOES.

A PAINTER outlines a picture. He prepares his canvas, then little by little develops the life he is calling into existence. Here a touch — bold, heavy, earnest; there, a delicate tracing so fine and perfect one would hardly know his pencil or brush had ever touched the canvas. And so, little by little, day after day, he studies, watching the effects of his labor, ever striving to reach into the ideal, which is the struggle of the soul after the perfection sometime to be its own. See

13

with what care, what pains, what delicacy of touch he lifts his dream to life. If it be a form, he makes the drapery, the face, the features, the very look — the thought — till at last his work is finished.

Then see how he cares for it, preserving it ever. He gives it light or shade — he gives it a frame and a place in his studio, where its beauties are ever before him, to please, to happify, to suggest, to build him up in the glorious existence which is his.

A bold, dashing lover wooes and wins. He talks, looks, acts love. He is at work on the heart of a woman — dearest of all pictures! He touches and colors by kind words — by smiles, by little attentions — by those little heaven-born endeavors which make woman to worship man, and man worthy the adoration of the pure, trusting, beautiful, loving, and virtuous. He wins by his boldness — his delicacy — his power to create new sympathies.

. . . .

The painter finishes his picture. He throws it by in disdain. It does not please him. He tosses it into a rubbish-room. Dirt and dust settle upon his work — it becomes torn, scratched, abused, till it is no longer a picture, but a daub worth less than the canvas on which it was painted. The creator becomes the destroyer, and a part of his own life is lost!

. . . .

The man who wooes and wins, is satisfied. He has won. The wife he sought is his. No more delicate touches — no more soul-warmed smiles — no more of that life-giving, protecting, heart-sustaining eloquence of living, which so beautifies the picture. He is now an owner — has a right to do as he pleases. He puts his picture, his wife, into a cold, unfurnished home — he tosses the rubbish of innumerable flirtations and adventures over her — he pours the slops of dissipation and debauchery over the

work he created — the heart he warmed into
life, and slowly destroys by neglect, cruelty,
and unkindness, the love he called forth, and
then blames the innocent picture for not retain-
ing its beauty, and its ability to win smiles and
words of approval.

As the skill of a painter gives life to his
work, so does kindness and careful love give
Heaven to united hearts. As each touch of
the brush calls forth some new beauty, some
new expression, some charming result ; so does
honest, noble, sober, manly love and devoted
honesty of heart and person beautify and spirit-
ualize united lives till there is before us a picture so good, so soul-resting, so complete in
its God-given sweetness that by this effort to
devotionalize our lives we rise above clouds,
storms, and temptations, and are given power
such as angels enjoy.

Thus are we inspired, ennobled, strength-
ened, and glorified in our natures by that Great

Power of Love Eternal, which rewards exactly in proportion to our allegiance, and made so strong for the good, that we live for centuries while the work we have planned is being done.

To preserve this picture the painter need not live in a palace — no more need the earnest man who would build himself into the beautiful Eternal by this simple caring for himself and his own. The frame need not be better than the picture — the home need not be more an object of thought than the loved one in your keeping. We may dwell in a hovel — may reside in a mansion; we only truly live in the heart.

If we surround ourselves with the good, the pure, the loving, the virtuous, the refined, the truly suggestive of the beautiful, we drink in of our surroundings and become day by day better and more deserving. Others cannot make us good, but they can help, and they will if we but show that we are deserving.

But if we do not try to improve and show

ourselves worthy the good opinion of real
friends, how can we expect them to take an interest in us. Those who sow little or much
care not to scatter by the wayside or on hills of
flint where the seed will die and bring no return.

.   .   .   .

Workingman — friend — brother. All the
day you have toiled in a shop, fashioning metal
or wood to certain designs. Or you have,
with aching back, fitted shoes to feet of horses,
that they might help man support his loved
ones. Or you have with rambling thoughts
followed the plow or swung the scythe till it
seemed as if the shade of yonder tree, the
draught from the spring; the drink from
the kettle, pail, or jug hidden under an armful
of new mown hay, were enough to tempt you
to abandon labor. Or you have all day in the
hot sun, with the perspiration streaming from
every pore, handled the ripe grain till the

beards on heads of wheat and barley have pricked you deep and sore.

Perhaps you have been at work in the woods, beating the march of civilization on the lofty pines and hard beeches, oak, and maples — with gleaming axes to the annoying tenor of stinging gnats and buzzing flies — working to build you a home and earn its adornment. Or you may have been all the day working in a mine — or sitting in your shop — or working at the case of types — or laboring anywhere by the day. No matter. You are our Brother. We are all workers together. We are all creators — each doing our best. You may pray on your feet, on your knees, or not at all, for this is your affair, not ours. But we are brothers, and we are, before God, your friend.

Come to our room and sit with us a few moments. Stay —'we will come to yours; this is better. Never mind the chair — we will sit here on this stool — this bench — this nail-keg upturned — this ·rustic seat, or on that log. It is late. In a few moments this week will have dropped into the silent well of time, never to be raised for our inspection till it comes with our record for His inspection. Soon you must sleep. Perhaps you are sleeping now. Then we will sit on the edge of your bed, no matter if it be but a·blanket on the ground or the floor.

This is your home. It is so much better than many have, we do not wonder you love it. The little one or ones sleeping just there are yours. In God's name, brother workingmen, do not throw these beautiful pictures you can so well finish, or certainly spoil, into the rubbish-room of neglect. That woman so tired, weary, overworked, and underloved is your wife — your darling. All the day long, and far into the night, has she toiled to help you. She is weary. We know it by her attitude in sleep — by the way her head is thrown back — by her heavy breathing, for thus do rest the weary and the overworked.

Look at the picture before you sleep. Do you wish her to love you better? Do you wish the little ones to be nearer and more loving? Do you wish your home to be more beautiful? Then listen, not to us, but to our good angel who to-night so smiles on us, and wishes us to talk to you for her. Fill your home with evidences of your loving care, and it will return to you an hundred-fold of happiness.

There is a place for a mat, or little piece of carpet. And there is just the place for a few shelves — a few books. And over there is a nice place for a little flower-pot. And there you can hang a bird-cage, or your little ones can train a vine.

You have no money? O, yes, There is money in your muscle! There is money in your brain. *There is honor in your heart.*

Work. Do not squander in dissipation. Do not throw your daily earnings from you to beautify the homes of others. You can do a little to-day — a little to-morrow — a little continually. And see how these littles will accumulate! Little acts of love — little words of kindness — little struggles to master yourself — little articles bought from small earnings saved will soon give you a more beautiful home — more happiness, more heart-rest, more strength, more honest pride, more manhood, more influence, more confidence in yourself, and more and more to you the deep, trusting, confiding love of your home ones.

Bear with others. Perhaps none of us are quite perfect. It may be that the ones we would find fault with, though not quite perfection, though very far therefrom, are as good as ourselves, and on the whole better than some others. It may be you are a painter. Then you try often, touching and retouching before the work is perfect. Perhaps you are a grocer, weighing out tea. Do you always throw into the scale the exact amount each time? You may be a tailor, or a dress-maker. Do you always give a perfect fit without the necessity of thinking and altering a little here and there? And if we cannot finish a picture at one stroke — strike the exact amount for a certain weight, or fit a garment the first attempt, how much less can we mold the inner life or outer life of a person to ours, at once, unless the Divine Builder has given us His aid?

Lead us not into temptation — *but deliver us from evil.* We are all tempted even as Christ was. We are at best but children who stumble, for ours is a rough road — but we can help others, who stumble, with us, to their feet, and not drag them down. Then we will all be better, and our lives will be to such purpose that our memories will not be tossed into the rubbish-room of forgetfulness, but will, reflecting

our lives, lead others to the beauties of the
Eternal Home beyond the threshold of our final
Saturday Night.

CHAPTER II.

WANTED TO GO BACK TO GOD.

O-NIGHT, when we passed out from our private office to call upon a lady friend, a pale-faced little girl at the foot of the street steps held before us a thin wooden board full of holes, nearly all of which held bouquets.

"Please, sir, buy a bouquet for your button-hole."

We looked at the tempting tea roses resting each on a leaf of geranium so sweetly — then at the poverty-stricken child before us, and wanted a bouquet at once.

"How much for this one, little kitten?"

"Ten cents, sir."

"Here is the money, and I hope you will sell all the rest before I return."

Then, with the little favor in a button-hole, we walked up town, passed the great hotels, through Madison square and on to our destination. Then we called on a Masonic brother in another part of the city — then to see a widow lady who had a sick child in hospital — then to a political club meeting, and when we had returned to the office to finish our week's work, it was past ten o'clock, and as the drowsy, old-time watchmen used to say — "All's well."

"Hello, little one !   You here still ?"

"Yes, sir, please."

"And not sold all your bouquets ?"

"No, sir, but I've tried to ever so hard."

"How many did you have ?"

"Fifty, sir."

"How many have you left now ?"

"Thirteen, sir."

"And it is past ten o'clock."

"Please, sir, I know it, but I have sold all I could."

"Why did you wait here?"

"To see you, sir."

"How did you know I would come back here?"

"I know you rooms here, sir — I've seen you come in very often."

"Which are my rooms?"

"Up there, sir, where the awnings are over the windows."

"What did you want to see me for?"

"Please, sir, I didn't know but you would want another bouquet; and I wanted to talk with you, sir."

"Talk with me! What about; and how did you know I would stop to talk?"

"Oh, sir, I knew you would. Sometimes my teacher, or the Superintendent, reads your

Saturday Night chapters in the Sunday-school, and we all know you there. And I knew you would, when you called me *little kitten* when you came out!"

"Well, little puss, come up-stairs. It is late, but you need not stay long."

Then we took out the great night-key to the heavy front-door, opened and entered. Then up the broad, solid stairway to our private rooms. In a moment the gas was lit, and the room was bright as day, and soon we sat in an easy chair by the desk, while the little bouquet seller sat on a little ottoman by our feet.

"Well, little kitten, what is your name?"

"Margy Radcliffe, sir."

"How old are you, Margy?"

"Nine years old, sir."

"Where do you live?"

"On Sixth avenue, near Twenty-first street, sir."

"Is your father alive?"

"Yes, sir."

"What does he do?"

"Nothing, sir."

"Is your mother alive?"

"Yes, sir."

"What does she do?"

"Nothing, sir, only sometimes she makes blue shirts for Mr. Waterman, who keeps a clothing store."

"Have you any brothers or sisters?"

"One little sister, six years old, sir."

"Where is she?"

"Selling flowers, too."

"Where do you get them to sell?"

"Of Mr. Klein."

"How much do they cost, each bouquet?"

"Six cents apiece, sir."

"Do you sell fifty each night?"

"Not always, but I try to. If I don't, father whips me."

"What for — what does he whip you for?"

"Because I don't sell them all!"

"Does he whip your sister, too?"

"Yes, sir, he whips us both!"

"Not very hard, I reckon?"

"Please, sir, look and see."

And we looked on the back and shoulders of the little one to see the blue marks where ugly blows had been by the dozen bestowed on the little girl who sat there in tears while her flowers were on the sofa beside us.

"If you do not sell all these to-night, will your father whip you?"

"Yes, sir."

"What time must you be home?"

"Any time before morning!"

"Does your father drink?"

"Yes, sir, every day!"

"Does your mother drink?"

"Yes, sir!"

"They do not both get drunk, do they?"

"Yes, sir; 'most every day."

"Is that the best dress you have?"

"Yes, sir, and the only one."

"How came you to go to Sunday-school?"

"A good woman, with a sweet face bought a bouquet of me last spring, and came to see me; and mother said I might go to Sunday-school."

"And you go every Sunday?"

"Yes, sir."

"That is right; I wish all the little children in the land could go. Why do you go?"

"To learn. And my teacher is so kind to me."

"Do you love her better than your father or mother?"

"Please, sir, I don't want to tell! But I don't love her better than Lotta, my little sister!"

And the tears ran down her face as she leaned forward and rested her head in our hand while we stroked the dust-filled hair which hung, but half combed, over her neck. Then she went to the wash-basin and gave her face a good bathing, wet her hair, and brushed it. Then we put some cologne on it, and she looked so unlike the tired little Margy who had been talking to us, that when she looked in the mirror she almost laughed.

Then she took a glass of ice-water and an apple from the fruit basket, and another one for her sister, and sat again on the ottoman to tell us what she wanted to when she waited for us.

And it was a queer wish. She wanted us to adopt her, or to find her a home somewhere, in some other city, where her father would not find her, and whip her so, and where her mother would not whip her every day. She told the story of her sad young life. Often had she been whipped, and sometimes brutally. She swept street-crossings in muddy weather, and sold bouquets, and picked rags, and so kept her parents alive and in drink. They lived in one little room 'way up-stairs, and never had butter on their bread.

Once her father was a merchant. Then he became a politician. Then he became a drunkard, and lost all his friends. And his wife took to drink, and so they drove their little ones to the street. God pity them — and all little children who have such parents.

She told us that life had no sunshine for her. No matter how well she did, cross words and blows were all the reward she had, till now, if we could not find her a home, she wanted to be sick and die, and go home to God, who, she said, she knew would not be so unkind to her! And the tears kept coming as she talked to us.

It was after eleven o'clock when she left, with all her bouquets sold. We went with her to the door, and let her out upon the street, when we saw her scamper away, glad to know that another night could she sleep on the floor without a whipping.

We were glad to make her happy, and are glad to know that so many children, who will read this, or whose father or mother will read it to them, have not such cruel, drunken parents.

In the great city are thousands of poor children who do not have even such homes as many poor children in the country have, and who would be very happy if they had nice beds and good food, and loving parents to care for them. We ask our little friends in the country to think of little Margy Radcliffe and her poor life, of her drunken parents and hard lot; and to see if they are not happy children, after all. They should be happy when their parents love them and care for them, as those who are good at heart always care for, or try to care for, their little ones and loved ones, as He who is our loving Father will care for us all, if we strive to be good, to be honest, true to ourselves and to do right.

And we who are older than children can think of her bitter young life already so sickening to her soul, that she longs to die and go back to God. And all of us who have little ones can resolve, that never will we thus forget our manhood, and be unworthy that beautiful rest with the loved ones in the Land of the Leal, when the week of life has gone, and we can, like the little waif whose story we have told as she told it to us, go to our rest with our work all done and no punishment to follow the blessed Saturday Night.

CHAPTER III.

ONLY THINKING.

E came to me in love — every word, every act, every move was to please. He spoke to me so kindly. He kissed me so tenderly. He brought me presents. He was always neat, clean, sweet, and cheerful. He seemed to live for none other than me. He wanted none other to speak to me — wanted me to speak to none other except with that cold formality which he taught me was queenly.

Loved him? I could not help it. Never had I seen a man so kind. He was unlike all others. When I rested my head against his breast, he was so careful where his hand wan-

36

dered — so gently would he bend to kiss my
brow — so smooth and gentle felt his hand to
my face — so expressive was the pressure of
his hand as palm rested in palm — so wildly
thrilling were those long, earnest, dreamy
kisses upon my lips like music of distant silver
bells or whispering murmur of low-singing
ripples; or like flutterings of beautiful coquet-
ting birds in the air, that I sank to sweeter
dreams in his embrace than ever before came
to me in hours of rest.

And, O! what castles in the air my fancy
built! He promised so much. His lips, his
eyes, his words, his touch, his look, his low
tones, his searching thoughts, his loving embrace, promised all in all to me. I asked for
no proof. Innocent, loving, earnest, believing
— thinking him the same, I said yes to his earnest wooing.

. . . It seems like a dream!

A horrid, ghastly dream. We were married. And how proud I was. In all the world no man like my adored. I would have followed him to death — to hell, because I was only happy where he was. There were but, two worlds to me. One was the heart-warmed spot where he was. A bright, golden atmosphere of love. A flower-filled garden, around which people might stand or walk — I cared not which. The other world was outside of this — all around it — where he was not. I lived within the golden-aired, loved-charmed circle. And I cared not who lived outside, so they did not break in to trample the flowers under my beautiful tree. I wanted not to go beyond to disturb those outside who might or might not have little bowers and gardens of their own.

. . . I was very happy. Others looked in upon our circle and envied us. . . One day tears came to my eyes. Perhaps I was foolish. I put my hand upon my heart and crowded it to silence, and looked about my beautiful garden. I had been mistaken. It was a garden after all. A bright, beautiful one. I would be happy. *I was happy.* . . He did not mean it. He came in from the world, and was cold. I would warm him to love — I did. He smiled as of yore. He kissed me as ever. I wept, and loved him the more. I was *so proud* that I had power over him and could warm his heart and kindle the fire in his eye.

. . . I rested in his arms. There was my place. I slept upon his bosom. I wakened in the night and felt for him — over there. I nestled to his heart. He turned away. Only sleeping nervousness. I kept still and listened to his breathing, and with careful hand lifted the coverlet to his throat that he might be warm. . . He wakened. He spake not as once. Then I blamed the world for dealing harshly with him — my loved. . . He turned from me and slept. His hand was not

so gentle as once.   His words were not so low-
toned.   His kiss lost its electrical velvet.   He
was heavy and thoughtless.   But he was mine,
and *I was content.*

. . . There came tears to my eyes. They
came from my heart.   Had I been dreaming?
No, I wept, and I slept.   I went down with
memory into the vapory amethyst of the past,
and visited with my love.   I felt again his
kiss — his touch — his presence.   I lived again
in the gentleness of his heart-lifting words.   I
wakened to think of him.   Perhaps I was ex-
pecting too much!

But he had promised even more!

And there came a mist — a faint, dim,
shadowy mist before my eyes.   It rested over
my little garden.   It reached from edge to
edge.   Faint, shadowy, almost transparent.
Others did not see it. . . It grew.   There
arose from it a form.   I stooped and looked
under it.   There was my lover — sitting as of

yore. My hand resting on his bosom. *I was content.* . . I chided myself for weeping, and rested with him. . . I looked again. The mist grew thicker. From where my lover slept there arose a form. A man. Slowly he came up. It was him I loved — yet it was not. I saw the change before the world did. I stepped into the mist. I clung to the changing form. I forgot all save life and my little garden. Still the mist thickened. The form grew. Colder, more stately. The dress was not that of my love. The hand was not his! The kiss was not his, but hurried, careless, unsatisfactory. His eye had lost its love-luster. It was simply the eye of a man. . . He spake and I listened. He commanded and I obeyed! He desired and I submitted! He feasted and I waited attendance in sickness or health. He walked to the wall and looked over into the world — I gazed at him. . .

The mist grew thicker. It hid my lover from

me. It became like a pavement, and under it
were my pretty flowers crushed with my air-
castles. . . . I felt a horror within me.
I will not tell you what or how. I cannot. The
ashes of unsympathetic desire poison deep and
lasting. . . . The horror became an agony.
The bosom I once rested so sweetly on, lost its
warmth. . . . I looked about my garden one
day to find its mossy banks turned to stone. I
was a prisoner! But not a murmuring one.
Still I was sad. I tried to be gay. He came
in from the world. Hither and yon. He came
with the flavor of other lips upon his lips.
. . . He came with an appetite gratified.
. . . The bouquet I had gathered for him
and culled the thorns therefrom, became a mat
at his door-step. Our garden was *his* at last.
. . . My heart grew sad and sore. The
walls to our garden grew higher. He stepped
upon my prostrate body, and then leaped the
walls to gardens beyond. He was my husband.

I was his wife. I saw changes and knew dreads
the world did not see or know, or it had pitied
me! . . The walls grew higher. The mist
grew colder. The one who arose therefrom
spoke to me — turned his heavy eyes upon me
— *I was dutiful!* . . I was too proud to cry
aloud. I had seen, and known, and felt what
others might have, or might not have felt. I
live to my duty. I dug under the frozen mist,
buried there all my olden dreams and memories. Others came and looked from the outside
of my prison walls to the within. They saw
something of the change, but could not see way
down to where my young life was buried. I
asked for pity. . . They told me martyrs wore
crowns. . . I asked for sympathy. They
said I had a protector. . . I asked for kind
words. . . They said I would find them in
my marriage certificate, which showed that I
was a legal wife. . . . They came to the
fence — to the wall and looked over. They

tossed me a volume of public opinion — a
prayer-book — a sermon — a congratulation
that I was a prisoner! He came and he went. He
commanded and I obeyed. He went and stayed
long. He came with hot breath, unsteady step,
coarse words, and brutal jests. His dress was
not that of the one I loved. He had no kind
words as then. . . . The flower was fair,
but the fruit! . . . Merciful God! . . .
Is this the dessert to the feast of early love?

. . . .

Yes! . . . I have! . . . And why
not? He broke *his* promises. He lived not for
me — he loved me not. He lied to me when he
won me, or he has so changed since that even
the world — his friends would not know him.
Our voyage was not to bring me to a prison!
I could have gone there alone! . . . I have
wept — and prayed — and waited — and hoped
— and forgiven — and watched — and striven
— and petted — and caressed — and trusted —

and struggled — and yielded — and suffered.
. . . But the man from the mist heeded not
— loved not! . . . Bouquets of thistles
and necklaces of serpents!

. . . Yes — and it is now too late. He
went and he stayed. One came and looked over
the walls to my prison home. He was not like
the one who went wandering away. . . .
His voice was kind. . . . I listened, and
it reminded me of the one who won my love
years ago! He spake and I listened, though I
tried not to! . . . O! the olden memories! . . . The olden hunger, when it comes!
. . . I could not go out — so he leaped the
wall and came to me! . . . There was no
one to love, to watch, to guard, to protect me.
O! had there been, he who came might have
looked over the wall — I should never have
seen him. . . . He smiled. He spake to me
kindly. He called up the olden memories, and
they came to his bidding. . . . What more?

I was dying of heart-hunger. And he fed me.
Perhaps it was poison, *but he fed me!* . . .
And *mine* would not. He was not mine, though
I was *his!* Yes — I *was* his — I am so still —
as much as he is mine ! I look not for his coming — I care not for it now. He may touch the
cords of the lute — but the music died out long
since. At least for him. . . . I did wrong.
. . . Why did they break the Sabbath when
Christ was on earth? . . . Because they
hungered ! . . . And how can a prisoner
have food except the keeper bring it? And
he brought it not. He bade me prepare feasts.
Yet brought me nothing ! . . . The world
condemns? Well — it may ! I am but human.
What else is the world? . . . "Lead us
not into temptation." But he who promised to
protect me led me there and left me ! . . .
Am I more to blame than he? A poor, weak,
trusting woman more to blame than man, who
is strong, and pitied, and excused? . . .

The blossom cannot combat the storm. The rill cannot defy the frost — nor the sun which comes after it. . . . The sunshine may not last forever — but it is sunshine. The cup may not be mine, but it gives life, and life even to a prisoner is something. If he who promised before God will not love me as each promised, am I bound by a contract he first broke? And must I starve, while he wanders to other feasting and self-inviting banquets? . . . — Thus ran her thoughts, as with head on her hand she sat thinking more of the past and present, than of this stormy, howling, tempest-driven Saturday Night.

CHAPTER IV.

WHAT WILL WE DO OVER THERE?

T is late, very late. Before this chapter will be finished, the day, the week will have gone, and another notch have been numbered on the scale of time.

But for a long talk this evening with an old friend we should have finished this chapter and our allotted work for the week, before this, and have written on another subject.

The friend who called was an earnest man. A deep thinker, though young as we count by years! He came and would not go till he had asked questions, and piled up, as it were mountain high, ideas, theories, and arguments.

" She sat thinking more of the past than the present."—*See page* 47.

He was afraid to die!

He wanted to know *why* he was. We told him all his fear was the result of pernicious education from the teachings of those who rule by fear, beneath a religion based on eternal, God-bestowing love! We pitied him. We pity any one who is afraid to go home! We pity the agent who cannot think without fear, of going to his employer. We fear that religion — that theory — that belief which teaches men to fear death. We would fear to love a tyrant!

All the land over are children being educated to dread death. Rather fear to live, lest we fail to live aright.

It is late and very still. Our room seems filled with a mellow, golden light — with smiles. The *presence* about us is beautiful beyond power of words. Our friend has gone. But we have something for him, for all who want more light.

4

This is an age of progression. Minds are bursting the fetters of ignorance and narrow superstition, as growing buds burst their pods; or growing trees burst the cords and ropes tied never so tightly around them by men.

Because this or that was of the past does not follow that it will be of the future.

The gas-burners overhead have taken the place of the saucerfull of fat with its floating cloth wick, by which we read years ago, as that took the place of darkness. The telegraph has killed the carrier-pigeon — the piano has taken the place of the harp — the engine has superseded the Ass on which He rode into Jerusalem — the little letters or types with which these words will be printed have superseded the hieroglyphics and mouth to ear traditions of those whose ashes have nourished trees, grown fruits — again enriched the earth and sprouted grass to again enrich roots and tint flowers.

These changes are the work of God. The plan of creation — continuing creation. As matter works upon matter, so mind upon mind. By chemical or other process the life of root, bark and leaf is extracted — the spirit is preserved, and remedies are made to be applied to those who are ill.

By the change called death the dross is removed, but the spirit is saved. Thus the Gardens of God in the wonderful Land of the Leal are filled with new-comers each day till in the Realms of Regeneration are multitudes no man can count — spirits in the Grand Treasure House, each to work for all time to come, but standing face to face and seeing no more of God Himself than we do here.

Why do we grow — expand, progress?

Why do plants grow in hot-houses? Why does iron take shape? Because worked upon by agencies — by a power irresistible. We teach children as those who have passed on to another sphere teach us. We are taught not alone by books nor by words. The winds, the storms, the light, the seasons, the events of time teach us.

Our minds are operated on. Not by minds here so much as by minds Over There, with power to reach us; to annihilate space — to teach us by thousands of agencies. As some speak in many languages while others speak but one, and that one poorly.

While on earth we have earth-born thoughts of earthly things. This is all there is of our present creativeness. Men make toys for children as other minds, older than ours, tell us of that life — not of earth and not known by us in the least unless we study, and ask, and are willing to be taught by those who alone can teach from works beyond our comprehension, but who do not care to teach those who will not learn.

There are workshops in the Eternal as here.

Minds working out great problems. Minds operating on minds by the power of that Eternal magnetic influence increasing there as the multitude increases in the spirit world or realm of improving minds.

All these inventions of the age are not alone of our planning! Others of the unseen are working with us. As we sit in our office in the East and direct agents, friends, mediums for working out our orders, miles and miles away in the West, so do thinkers, planners, suggesters, inventors, teachers and helpers of struggling humanity, out of sight and circles away in advance of us, work through us, with us, and for us, as for themselves and for the grand labor of Creation which was not ended when the world was, as some say, finished.

The world is not finished!

It never will be. And there are millions of unfinished worlds. There are workers there, doing something of which we may know all in time as we progress, fit ourselves and are fitted by teachers who have passed the threshold before us, and who will aid us if we will it so.

In the Eternal will be, and are, workers for good and for evil. Two opposite spirits — forces, powers. Two opposing principles. If we are pure, loving, earnest workers here, careful to preserve our manhood, and to progress in labor, intellect, goodness, and high attributes, we shall, Over There, be with and work with the pure, the kind, the beautiful in spirit, the loving, and the ones who benefit those ever to be educated.

The beauty of the Eternal work will be our Heaven. The reward there, as here, when we see our plans prosper, our ideas take root and grow, our labors adding to the happiness of others. And this will be Heaven.

If we are not pure, and loving, and true to that great God-like principle of purity while on earth, we will enter the Eternal Gardens the

same, and will have no place prepared for us —
no beautiful welcome from the pure; sweet
there, as welcomes here are sweeter from the
pure and the good, more than from those who
are not. Then will come a realization of lost
opportunities in not fitting ourself by good lives
and good deeds while at school on earth.
The work on which the good will ever be
engaged will be work those who are not good,
and pure, and earnest, and loving, and liberal,
and truthful, while here taking lessons, will
not be fitted for.

Then will come to them remorse of con-
science — regret to know and to feel that they
are in the Land of the New Life without capital,
or credit, or a name, or a demand for them
with the workers for the good. And this will
be their agony — their hell.

And their lives must be lived over again
under teachers and under restraints till again
shall they pass on, but far in the wake of those

who are worthy and continually called to higher planes and greater teachings, as far beyond our present comprehension as algebra is beyond the ken of babes, or the science of phonography is beyond the rude symbolizings of savages.

Thus believing — thus taught by those who so often come to us with news from those who have gone before us — thus educated by unseen teachers who daily give us lessons and proofs of all this of which we write, death has no more terror for us than has the sleep we shall soon lie down to. We have no fear of hell, for the worst of our life is passed, as with all who are progressive. Others may not like our faith, but it is good enough for us to live by — it is all the faith we want to die by. Death, as you call it, has no terror for us, for long since have we lost the fear thereof.

Only do we ask to live to a purpose — to do good — to help make others happier — to combat error — to thrust our pen into the darkness, like that within the inkstand before us, that light may follow. Only do we ask to live here for those who love us and whom we love, caring nothing for the speech of those who do not love us — caring only to do our duty — to live a good life — to help others — to give comfort to those in darkness, waiting for the light which will soon come to all on earth, as will come the rest, the dawn, the Sabbath morning after shall have faded out and passed away the darkness of Saturday Night.

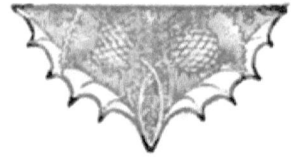

CHAPTER V.

A LIFE LOST!

BEFORE us is a letter opened not an hour since. The echoes of the silent words it contains are reverberating down and through the corridors of memory — waking echoes on the points and in the valleys of the road to the river long since passed. We have been thinking of the contents of the letter. Not a tear has fallen, but a great welling sensation of the heart — a silent reaching back, as if to recover that part of life's chain which is slipping from us, seven links a week — to look at a portion thereof again.

. . . . . . By the way, Mrs. ——, she whom you know was Maggie ——, died Saturday night last, and was buried this afternoon. Poor woman — I could not help weeping like a child as I stood and saw her coffin settling to its resting-place. And I must not forget to tell you, for *you* too knew her and will drop a tear over her unhappy memory.

Gone Home! O! Father, we thank Thee, and not one single tear holds back or gives weight to the kindly greeting we send in thought, from the heart on the sunshine, over the humanity-filled river which marks the boundaries of here and there!

Poor Maggie here — happy Maggie there. Would you care to know of her? We will tell a little chapter of life-history, woven by the longings of the soul — burned by tears into the vail so many wear, to keep their hearts from the eyes of those who cannot penetrate to the beyond.

Years ago we knew her. A beautiful girl budding into womanhood. Did we love her? Others did, for hers was a soul and a heart worthy all love. One who loved her, with her

wondrous eyes and beautiful golden hair, was a
friend of ours. A noble-hearted, brave, earnest
young man, whose life was like glass, clear, for
all men to see through. A thousand hearts in
one not richer than his in manly worth, impulses noble, and purpose of ambition honest,
and boldly reaching high above and beyond
those who little reflect. But he was poor in all
save pluck. No heart and hand more quick or
open to the needy in weakness or affliction.
'Twas he that loved poor Maggie, and never
were mortals better mated to make life's pathway smooth, and bring happiness each to the
heart of the other.

But to them the future was dark — perhaps
because his faith did not reach through the
gloom to the golden-lined success, waiting his
winning. He trembled between hope and fear
— between storms of heart and brain, as does
the leaf, when counter currents toy with its fee-
bleness. He lacked the bold earnestness and

manly daring to take her to himself, and swim steadily, battling the waves, till the beautiful island in the sea of life was reached. He feared to lose her, and so fearing, lost her forever, and down the tide of time swept her heart and their happiness, as merry laugh of child is borne to the dark home of the tempest in the stormy hours of night. He did not know how stout of heart, brave of soul, glorious in trusting confidence, a woman can be when wholly loved by an honest heart, no matter how closely poverty keeps vigil and guard. Nor did he know that love, patience, and economy will sooner or later drive the gaunt sentry from its post.

And Maggie? Those who held restraint parental over her life and heart said to her that she must not marry one who was poor. They told her she had been educated to grace the parlor. They told her she must not wed the youth who loved her, and whose heart with hers speeded joyously, lightly, trustingly together far out in that ocean of happy life, beckoning them to follow hand in hand. They told her, while her poor heart was breaking, that it was her *duty* to marry to please her parents. That they knew better than she what she wanted. As if other than God or the one chosen by sympathetic nature can read the heart!

And poor Maggie, "like a dutiful girl," drank the poison of parental interference, buried her heart beneath its dead hopes, gave her hand to the choice of those who were murdering her, and with her education, her love all dead, became the wife of another, who had wealth and friends of influence, and who told her she *must* wed him or he would die, and his death would rest on her soul. As if one who would thus demand could really love a woman and make her happy!

Years fled as if affrighted. The proud young man, who so loved the beautiful girl for her heart and trusting goodness, died, risking his

life, at Fredericksburg. 'Twas there they found
him, his forehead pierced by a musket ball,
asleep; the clotted blood hiding the face. A
litle locket suspended by a golden chain from
his neck hid the features of the only one he
ever truly loved — poor Maggie, who was doing
her *duty* as the wife of another. God rest him,
and her, in the mellow sunlight of united love
amid the ever-blooming flowers of the beautiful
Eternal. Do we mourn her death — her *life*
you mean? No!

She lived for duty. 'Twas a broken heart
and a passive hand she gave another. He married her for her beauty. Those who marry for
this roam for the same!

The years came and the years went. She
lived in a "home," but in it was little sunshine
for her. She tried to do her duty. She tried
to love him. He was kind to her as goes the
world. He surrounded her with luxuries —
with pride presented her as his wife. He was

proud of her beauty, and felt safe to leave her with others, for he knew her life was cold, passionless, unmoved by love. By this he trusted her. Not like one whose soul is filled with that grand, deep, wondrous love that so takes to itself a kindred soul and defies the world to step between or to win away from that God-blessed allegiance which is oil upon the waves of the dark river, that those who love truly may pass over to the flower-lined shores, untossed, unharmed, unseparated!

But poor Maggie. Her life was not thus. He drank of her beauty, then quaffed from other cups. He held her by cable of iron and anchors of ice. She was *his wife.* He came and went. When he took her, the ruins of her only love were upon the grief-wrapped altar of her heart, and its portals closed — he could *never* enter to the mellow warmth, the life-giving beauty, the crowning happiness of mortality. He could only live outside, receiving

the kindness of a noble woman, from her con-
sciousness of his *claim*. And she lived. God
alone knows how. Her life grew almost insup-
portable; to be daily, nightly, subject to the
intimate companionship of a being whose
coming she dreaded — whose kiss chilled her
very soul — whose touch was agony — whose
passionate embrace a painful, sickening, disgusting horror! But she lived to her duty
like one who walks to martyrdom. In his
presence her tired heart shrank away like the
drop of dew caught by the frost. But she was
doing her duty! She was dying by inches.
Her murderers were proud of her. The breath
of scandal never swept her down. She was a
model wife. Cold, distant, indifferent. Her
smile was fitful, like the sunbeam of autumn
flying before the wind, as if in terror hastening
homeward, or anywhere to escape.

She did her duty! She cared for him in
sickness without murmur. And when from her

nursing came health, he roamed for beauty;
and wasted his strength in lifting other goblets
to his lips. Her home was her prison. But
she lived for her duty! Oft did she wish to
escape — to go out into the world — to the
grave of her dead love, anywhere rather than
walk in Siberian torture. But no! The world
stood before her like an army of savages with
uplifted weapons to beat down whoever would
run the gauntlet from bondage to freedom —
from misery to happiness. The world can pray
and advocate for liberation of laborers from
protected servitude, then dance in glee around
the pyres whereon are burning sorrow-laden
hearts, and call this unspeakable torture, Christianity!

She longed to take back to herself the
wreck of her hopes, to go alone to the grave
of her life, and look over its withered leaves;
she longed to escape the torture only women
held like her can feel; she longed to escape

the cold, indifferent, unloving, heart-destroying tyranny of "home;" to find some one to love who would love her; to live a life of usefulness and prepare for Heaven — but no! Bigotry, puritanism, fanaticism, ignorance, narrow-minded illiberality waved its banner from door of church and the corrupt society that there find such frequent cover, and the cohorts of despotic tyranny sprang to toss back into freezing waters the poor, heart-wrecked unfortunate, thrust therein by authority and forms ceremonial, only to sink to the bottom, content with doing a Christian duty.

So lived poor Maggie. So she died. Her life was lost. Not when the kind angel caught her prayer, and bore it with her sorrowed soul to brighter scenes, but when she followed duty to the prison cell wherein her heart was locked and kept a freezing prisoner. Her life was a failure. She marked no happy result. Her life was not a beautiful flower to adorn and

beautify. She was cowardly, but the world
that stood with hot tongue and bitter-pointed
pen in front of her prison to terrify, defame,
and pierce through the one who, but for this
inhuman cowardice, might have been happy,
is a million times more so. And so to-night
we have been thinking. Poor Maggie went
home a week since. Her Saturday Night came
and brought her joy at last. We are glad.
Her life was lost years ago.

O! kind Father in Heaven, wilt Thou not
lead her to its return in the beautiful Land of
the Leal, where Christianity is different from
that called Christianity here? She was good
here. She gave strict obedience to her parents.
She knelt with them in childhood, and grew to
womanhood on the cold, heartless, unchristian,
illiberal barren of mistaken duty, as if GOD,
who is all goodness, asks those who come to
His breast to come with dead hearts, trembling
spirits, dread and disgust of the present life,

which is to fit us for happiness hereafter, in proportion as we are truly happy, deserving and liberal.

Some day we will plant a flower over the bed where sleeps the one whose life was lost — who was held by her parents and her husband, while a Christian world did with devilish satisfaction most brutal murder.

And we will plant a flower there which will grow to shelter the thousands and tens of thousands of heart-wrecked women of the land, who, following a line of mistaken duty, with grief-strained hearts, trembled before an illiberal world, and follow their so-thought destiny to a grateful grave. We know there are thousands of them, and know that a more liberal morn is breaking. It is not the duty of any person to make him or herself miserable. It is this mistaken idea which is demoralizing society. The doctrine that women must live simply to a duty — that that duty is to live with tyrants, brutes, despots, filthy forms, and those whose touch is agony — whose caresses are only for self-gratification — whose hearts blend not with hearts simply because the world so edicts, is filling the land with sorrow, criminality, and reckless search after happiness in paths where it is seldom found. Exclude the light from a plant, and it dies. Let light in from only one direction, and the vine reaches its pale tendrils toward the blessing. So with the heart. If there be no light of love completely surrounding it, there will be reaching out this way and that to find that which is in reality all there is of life, as it is the great basis of His mercy, power, and goodness.

God rest the ones whose lives were lost. And may the thousands everywhere who read this be happier than was she who sleeps now in a country churchyard. May parents not murder hearts. May men not demand sacrifices which will rust their souls, and may all the young who would be happy find as true hearts as had the one who lay down to his rest on the field of battle. And to those who, like poor Maggie, are tied to a devilish, heart-torturing duty; may they dare step out from life-losing bondage, take back their own, and teach men that though woman be weak, she can be strong in this her great protection, while waiting for joys in the Island of Rest, where the sun is Love, the Christianity liberal, and there never comes for the soul the darkness of a Saturday Night.

CHAPTER VI.

TO A POOR LITTLE BOY.

THIS stormy Saturday night, as we were on the street, with a protector from the rain, looking in at the shop windows, at the beauty and the brightness therein displayed; then at the storm evidences and darkness outside, and thinking how much like life was all this, a poor, little, ragged newsboy came up to us.

But first, our musing over the light within, and the darkness without. Some one had lit the lights and lamps within, and all was brightness. Without these lights all would have been darkness in these now beautiful shops, And so with us all. The lamps of love — the

72

light of kindness and good-nature we keep in our hearts, make us happy — make others happy, and no matter how the storm of life may rage outside, all is cheery within, and friends come to rest with us.

The little newsboy. He was a ragged little fellow, for he had no home, as have thousands of the boys who read this. His feet were bare and blue, for the weather is cold. The rain dripped from the bottom of his ragged vest and pants, and beat in through his torn cap, to moisten his nut-brown hair, so soft and glossy.

We did not know him — but he knew us, as witness the following well-remembered conversation.

"Good evening, Mr. Pomeroy. Will you have a paper?" And he handed us one yet damp from the press.

"Certainly. How many have you yet to sell?"

"Nine more — I have sold forty-one now."

"Well, here is the money for all you have left. And if you can sell all but this one again, do so."

"Thank you, sir. And please, sir — will you do me a favor, sir?"

And he looked up so honest and earnest, who could help answering promptly, —

"Certainly, my little friend, if it be possible. What is it?"

"Well, sir — I don't know as you will, but I wish you would write just one 'Saturday Night' chapter for me! I would rather you would than give me a new suit of clothes!"

"Write a 'Saturday Night' for you? What shall we say? Perhaps our good angel will not be willing?"

"Oh, yes! It seems as if she would, or I never would have come and asked you! I will keep it, and *some day* will thank you for it if I live."

O! the beauty and the strength of *perfect*

faith. " Ask and ye shall receive " came to us, and we told the little fellow we would. Then he bade us good-night and went his way, while we walked on in the rain, our heart as light and cheerful as the most beautiful of all the places we passed and peered into through unblinded windows.

.   .   .   .

— *Saturday Night to a little Newsboy.*

God love the earnest little fellow — and all the earnest little boys in the world. We will write for him and for them, if they will come and sit here in our, pleasant room. It is not large, but millions can sit with us, and the golden presence which so mellows our life and makes us happy, will touch them all, to warm, to gladden, to beautify, with that wondrous power would to God all might possess.

And now, little fellow, sit right here on this ottoman, whereon many and many a heart-broken sufferer has sat to tell us her or his story. Sit there, so we can look into your eyes, and we will talk with you.

You are a poor little boy. A homeless wanderer. One that is almost forgotten. So were we once, and thus having been, we will talk very plainly and kindly to you to-night, just as a gentle presence so often by day and by night — when the heart was full of doubt and storm — talked with us till happiness came to her bidding.

You wish to be a man? Then you can be. The future is before you, ready to unfold beauties if you earn them. What if you are poor now? You can be good, and the rich can be no more! You can work and you can win. In time you can become a leader among men. And if you cannot lead, you can follow, till others see your good qualities, and put you ahead.

Only be honest. Be kind. Do not be coarse and vulgar, for thus is your heart deadened, as the rust which marks where lemon-juice rested on the steel blade spoils its beauty and weakens it forever. Be kind to those who are poor and weak. See how much you can do well each day. See how much you can learn. See how much you can do each week that you will feel satisfied with. And do not fret, nor give up. Boys who thus act are poor timber, and soon break.

What if some boy is better dressed, and sneers at you? Pass him by; it is hard to tell who will win the race. Suppose that boy rides in a carriage. Thank God you have health to walk and run, and some day you can ride if you will. See how much of a little man you can be; and some day we will see how much of a great man you are. And, above all, be honest and be prompt. Never refuse to do a favor when you can, even to an enemy, if the favor be based on the right. And do not be envious of others, for envy curdles the young life to make an unhappy old age.

Keep on trying. Many have failed, but others have won. Do your work willingly, and never, *never*, NEVER be afraid or ashamed of work. GOD Himself was a worker — behold what He did! And we who would succeed must work and wait; the good seed sown to-day brings its reward all in due time.

Sometimes, my little boy, the days will be dark, and it will seem such hard work to wait. You will imagine others to be doing better than yourself. Very likely; but are you not doing much better than many others? And you must try to do even better than the best. And so the years will come and go. And friends will come — never to go if they be friends, and you be deserving. Each day, each week, each month, each year, will find you stronger, and braver, and better, and richer, and more loved, and happier, as you will add to your influence and use it for the right.

Honors will follow confidence. As you respect yourself, others will respect you. As you strive to be somebody, others will help you, for you then can help them! You will live to see many of the rich boys you envy go to wreck and to ruin. You will see poverty, following dissipation, take them to its embrace, and rest with them in the gutter, where the smiles of friends are not known. You will see the grave close over the forms of those who, unlike you, have no self-respect, no pride, no wish to be good, or great, or powerful. And each year you will be more loved as you are good and deserving. And you will look back with such earnest pride to your own success, — to the loved ones about you — to the conquests you have made — after first learning to rule and govern yourself.

Thus and thus only will your life be a success. It is easy to be a loafer — to be a drunk-ard — to be a coarse, careless, brutal man; but, my little boy, you can be so much more if you will. Years have we lived,— long labor-giving years, — but never have we seen a poor boy long friendless, or a deserving man long out of a situation. So try earnestly, and some-body will help you — somebody will love you — somebody will be proud of you, and your life will be beautiful.

We wish all the little boys in our great coun-try would try to be good men — to be sober, earnest, deserving men. Some of them will, and some of them will not. Those who try will be loved, and happy. Those who do not will never know the real helping support good lives and good actions bring, but will drop by the wayside into pine-coffins, shallow graves, weed-covered burial-places; unhonored, and soon for-gotten.

While those who are good and who strive

earnestly will be men of wealth, of power, of worth, of influence. They will help make laws, for the days of bad law-makers in this country are passing steadily away. And they can do good, and at last, when they have won victories here, have conquered obstacles, and been rewarded on earth, will be so trained, purified, and made useful, that there will be given to them great works and less labor, over the River in the Land of the Leal, where beautiful Groves, and harmonious Homes, and Eternal Love will hold all who are good, as we pray sweet sleep to fold in her careful embrace each and every one who reads this well-meant ending of the week and of Saturday Night.

CHAPTER VII.

THE BEAUTY OF LIFE.

EVER so blessed a Saturday Night as this came to us before. Perhaps you do not care to read this, which some may call but sentiment. But it is life.

All the week we have been so happy. Every day a day nearer. Every week a shortening of the time so long a-coming. The watch open before us ticks the seconds — chips from the block of God's time — into the well of the past, as drops fall from an ascending bucket. And the crystal drops not purer than we are happy to-night, for the week just ending bears more than one record of good, and not one of intentional wrong.

And we are happy to-night, for she, too, is happy. And would you know who she is? We will tell you if you care to know.

One day — oh, long ago — if days or weeks, or months, or other notches of time were centuries, we met her. A pure, loving, trusting, earnest woman, whose kind words warmed our soul, and whose trusting smile, so heaven-lit, seemed such a protection. All the day and the days had we been tempted; it seemed beyond our strength. Others had turned against us. Others had spoken bitter, cruel, cutting words, perhaps because, not guided by the same light, they did not see as we did, and not know our motives. Before it seemed as if the world had all gone wrong. And as the shadows darkened over our heart, to crush, to deaden, to destroy — as dissipation opened wide the portals to bid us enter, she came between us and ruin with the Heaven-born protecting love of purity, kindness, confidence, and that deep perfection of love which casts out fear, and so gives strength to good resolves and impulses for the right. . . .

And often has her love been our shield from life's storms. When tempted to dissipate, to squander, to *forget*, her love-lit eye, her trusting, earnest, heart-reaching look has come to us. In dreams she has been beside us — in the hours of the day and the night her words and smiles have been with us.

When we tried to do right she always encouraged. When we were wrong, she came with gentle hand, to rest us with her velvet touch. When others looked bitter, she looked sweet — tenfold so as we turned to her with a heart all her own, for life or death.

She is and always has been good to us. She believes in us. She trusts us, and God knows we would not deceive her. She has an influence over us — and knows it. So she exercises it only for the good, the pure, the noble.

We talk with her. We tell her all. The grave is not closer than her lips when the secret of another is behind them. We live in her love, grow strong in her faith, and are happy because entirely content. We have no fears she will forget us or fail to love. We have no fears that *any one* can win her, for we defy any one, except aided by God's great power, to come between us — to separate us.

She is good, and kind, and pure, and so we love her. If she were not thus to us she would trifle with us, and then our love would be lost.

. . . .

Every day do we have evidence of her love and care. She did this to-day — that yesterday, and that the day before, to aid us both — to make us happy. She fixed that article; she arranged those; she makes our little room so homelike; she leaves the imprint of herself on each book, picture, flower; each little gift, keepsake and memento in the room, as her little work, so neatly done, was to add to our happiness and the beauty of our home.

I am proud of her, of her love. I am honored by her trust in me. I have faith in her love and her protecting influence. I know she is the best friend I have on earth; that to her I owe so many, many hours of happiness.

And as I am happy in this true, pure, earnest love, so am I earnest in its defence. My heart is so full of golden-hued sunshine. Every day I try more and more to be good, to be kind; to do some good, and to live to some purpose. And the more I try the more I succeed, and the happier we both are. She is the queen and I am the subject. Here she rules better than with the ballot, for now my pride is to protect her, thus growing stronger myself. Yet she does vote. My heart is the ballot-box, her eyes the voters, her kind words the ballots, with not one against me from week to week, from month to month.

. . . .

And I feel so proud to know that I am a kind, loving, earnest, darling-loving working-man. I am proud to think I am worthy the love of a good, pure, virtuous woman, whose heart and mine each year run more and more together as our lives ripen for a pleasant hand-in-hand walk through all the groves of God in the beautiful Land of the Leal. Others may dissipate and waste their strength, but while she loves me I cannot fall — *I will not.* So says that good spirit which for so many years has been with us — which has led us back with her oft and oft, to that Loving Presence *which has promised us* sweet rest with those we love when comes our call from labor to refreshment.

I have her love, as she has mine — all and complete on earth — united as it will be over there where there will be no sex; for those who will reach there will be so blended and united that the perfection not ours to enjoy on

earth will then be given us. I have her word
as she has mine — her vows as she has mine. I
fear no seducer or debaucher, for our love and
honor is too perfect for anything to separate.
And thus we are worthy of each other.

And worthy of the dear home we have. Of
the good friends we have. Of the happiness
we enjoy. Our home may be small, but it is
our home. It may be in the city or forest, but
it is ours. Others' may not love us, but we
love each other, and what more did Father and
Son do while in Heaven together, or while
separated for a short time.

And she I love so well may not be the richest woman in this world's goods, but she is the
best, the truest-hearted, and we are growing old
together, nearing our meeting in the Golden
Beyond. She may smile on others, but her
sweetest smiles are for me. No one watches
over me as does she. No one so ready to forgive as she, except it be He who forgives us

all. The more we do for each other, the more happiness we find therein — for thus do good endeavors come laden with sweet perfume. And though I am but a workingman, I am very, very happy, for I am content to love as Christ loved us all, and in this contentment willing to labor, and help make others happy. As we all hope to be when the tired head is pillowed on the mossy bank over there — where we will live in the love of our loved ones and mingle with those who on earth knew and enjoyed true manhood and the society of the good. May we all live here so that we may enjoy the pure after there comes to us golden dawn, which soon will come, following the blessed Heaven-opening Saturday Night.

CHAPTER VIII.

ONLY A WIDOW!

O-NIGHT we stood in front of a house, watching a woman at work. The curtain not quite down, but we could look in and see a woman at work. One of God's toiling millions here at her task long after nightfall. Had she known we were there, she might have thought us impertinent — but we did not mean to be so!

She swept the floor — no carpet thereon. She set the chairs in place — shoved a little table to one corner of the room. Then she stopped before a glass to smooth her hair back from a brow that seemed to us fair, but sorrow-lined. Then she stirred up the fire, took a lamp from the mantle, and set it on a little table close by a sewing machine, and soon was at work, although it was three hours past sundown this Saturday Night, as she worked and we watched.

"Hello! is that you?"

"Yes."

"What are you standing so still for?"

"Looking at that woman — you can see her, look under the curtain."

"Only a poor widow at work — what sense in looking at her? Come along — I'm going your way."

And so we reeled up our thread of thoughts, and walked homeward to the little room where we sit to write this chapter, and wait to say good-by to the week, for we shall never see it again, and would part friends.

Only a widow!

And is not that a volume? You who see

only a widow at work, see not the hundredth part. We see a woman whose life may have been happy — may have been miserable. If happy ——

She had a home. She was loved and petted and cared for and protected and caressed by one who was dearer to her than all others. She was one who to his manly keeping had confided her love, her heart, her affection, her life. To aid him who is now mourned was her delight. To care for him — to welcome him home from toil — to watch by and over him in sickness — to lighten his load, minister to his wants, and make him proud *of* her, happy *with* her, earnest and manly through her, was her great, noble, God-given mission.

We looked back to the days when she gave her heart and herself wholly to him. To the time when the two started out as young voyagers on the sea so full of wrecks. We saw him bending to kiss her — holding her to his heart — smoothing back the hair from her forehead— looking 'way down the mystic depths of those loving eyes, into the heart all his own — sitting side by side, palm in palm — resting his tired head on her bosom, or hers on his — kissing her and calling her his darling.

And we saw the years fading as they followed the vapory weeks down the vale of time. And age leaving marks and furrows on their brows, as occupants of cradles came to bind them still closer in love and life. And we saw with what pride she looked on him; good, true, noble, loving, kind-hearted man and considerate husband; affectionate and honest parent, setting good examples, as he would make of his sons and daughters *men* and *women*.

And we saw the house growing in its attractions — friends calling to enjoy their hospitality — the walls being covered with pictures — the rooms everywhere adorned with articles of lux-

ury, taste, comfort, and convenience. We saw
their home becoming happier as they learned
how little the world cared for them and how
much they cared for each other — how happy
were they together, how nervous, uneasy, and
lonely when separated. How she watched for
his coming — greeted him with a kiss — how
he held her to his heart and rested from his
labor in her loving presence.

Then we saw her watching over his sick bed
— her heart in fear, tears, agony, and then they
told her he was dead — and *then*, like a dream
went her life of happiness, and she was at sea,
alone, hopeless, heart-wrecked, living on the
floating, tear-wet memories of the happy past.
The good ships parted company before the golden shore was reached — she is left to sorrow
and to sink — to labor and to repine — to struggle through the waves of affliction with her
weary load till death comes to her relief.

Only a widow !

Great God! As if that were not enough. And you all speak unkindly of her, as if his death were her crime! You shut her out from employment — you compel her to work for pennies where you pay others dollars — you take delight in giving her work, and cheating her out of her scanty pay — you deem it Christianity to torture and overwork her, for she is only a widow!

If her heart from its despair turns to the light of kindness and loving words — if she smiles on one who speaks kindly to her — if she dares raise her eyes from the grave of her lost one, the young and old alike sneer at her, for she is only a widow. And she struggles on with wondrous heroism. She cares for her little ones. She does her duty. She takes still closer to her heart the little ones he left, and then you blame her for loving her first-born — the ones who are warmed by the sunlight of olden mem-

ories of *him*, no matter how changed her life
may be.

God love all the widows — all who have lost
their loved ones — all who are sorrowful of heart
for those who sleep here to waken just over
yonder! We love the earnest men with wives
and little ones, who strive to live loving, useful lives. We love the men who labor, and
plan, and take care of their homes and earnings,
that their widows and their children may not
come to want and be driven from sorrow to
suffering all the years to come. We love the
men who are kind to the widows — the women
who care for them and speak kindly to them —
the society which gives them employment and
good pay — the men who love their wives well
enough to care for them — to provide them with
a home, as every man does and will do who
really loves the woman of all others he pro-
fesses to love most. We love the man who,
reading this, thinking of the past and of his

"On the bed lay the little girl we came to see."—*See page* 99,

loved ones, dare deny himself dissipation, and dare labor earnestly, that his wife may love him better here, and his widow may not suffer should he be first called to rest, leaving her a load of sorrow to bear from his Eternal morn till her final Saturday Night.

7

CHAPTER IX.

PATIENT IN SUFFERING.

SOME weeks ago one of the men working in our office told us of a little girl who the day before had fallen down stairs and broken her hip. Said he : —

"It is too bad, for she was such a playful little romp, and her mother is too poor to care for her as she should be cared for."

So we went out with him one night after the day's work was done. Down a narrow street, turning here and there — into a cross street swarming with noisy children, dogs, cats, and jostling humanity. Then into a little alley between two brick houses — into a little back yard or area lined by house walls — up the back stairs one, two, three flights — into a little half-furnished room.

Only one room, not twenty feet square. Two windows looking out into, and down upon the contracted area or yard. Not a bit of carpet on the floor — one little ten-cent picture (a little girl playing with a kitten) on the wall — a little, old, cracked stove in a corner, with a stew-pan thereon, in which a bone was being boiled. A rude bedstead stood in the opposite corner, three old chairs and a three-legged table standing against the wall, marked the comforts of this "home." By the table, working by the light of a small kerosene lamp, sat a middle-aged woman, making blue overalls, while on the bed lay the little girl we came to see.

" And here is where you live ? "

" Yes, sir — we try to live here."

" How is the little one to-night?"

" Just about so, sir. She suffers a good deal."

" She bothers you about working, does she not?"

" Yes, sir, but I don't mind that."

" How many hours a day do you work?"

" I don't know, sir. I am up as soon as it is light, and I work all day till everything is still on the streets; about midnight, I think, sir."

" What rent do you pay for this room?"

" Two dollars a week, sir."

" How much do you earn?"

" Sometimes sixty cents a day. But since Annie has been sick I can't earn more than fifty cents, and some days not that."

" You can't lay-up much, then?"

" No, sir. It is hard work to get along. When Annie is well she makes some days ten cents selling papers, and if it is too rainy to sell papers she sweeps the crossings."

"How much does she make rainy days?"

"Some days nothing. Some days a few pennies. Once a man gave her a dollar, and I got her a new dress with it, and some shoes at a second-hand store. Once a lady gave her a half a dollar, but such things don't happen very often."

"Have you a husband?"

"Yes, sir — but, sir, he only comes here to sleep, and sometimes does not come at all. Sometimes he is here to supper and to breakfast — sometimes he comes here when he is sick."

"Don't he help support you?"

"Not now, sir. He used to, but he don't now, sir. He takes what money Annie makes, and goes off with it when I don't have a chance and take out part of it, and then he scolds and swears at me."

"What does he do for a living?"

"Nothing, sir. He goes around; I don't

know where. He is off with somebody, and drinks a good deal, sir. Sometimes he don't come home for a week."

"Do you love him?"

"Yes, sir — I *did* love him once, but it seems a long while ago, sir — when we lived in Harlem, and began to keep house, and when Annie was born. But he is not now as he was then, sir. Then he was good, and never struck me, sir."

"He does not strike you now, does he?"

"Sometimes, sir, but not often. Only when he is in liquor. Two weeks ago he struck me with a chair because I did not have anything for him to eat, and I was lame a good while so I could not lift Annie, but it's most well now."

And she showed us a long, greenish-looking bruise on her left shoulder, yet painful to the touch.

"Don't he help take care of Annie?"

"No, sir. He scolded when she fell down

stairs, and said she was careless. And that is all he does."

" Has he been home to-night ? "

" No, sir, not yet. He may come any minute."

" Let us see about the little one. How old is she ? "

" Eight years last July, sir."

Then we sat upon the edge of the rickety bed and looked at the little girl. A pale, feverish, little bundle of nervousness and aching pains. She lay in bed, a bundle of old rags under her head — the jet black hair in striking contrast with her pale face. An old shawl was thrown over her as she lay there helpless, her eyes looking at us as we have seen lambs look when waiting the knife of the butcher. We felt her wrist — it was hot, and the pulse was unsteady. Her brow was hot with nervous fever. A coarse under-garment revealed the half-starved anatomy before us, as she seemed to say — "Please sir, I can't help being poor, for my father don't love me!"

We looked into her eyes till the tears came — till the lashes over hers closed, and she turned her little head to the wall, while the tears trickled down her face.

"Annie! Look here, little one."

Slowly she turned, —

"Please, sir, I didn't mean to cry, but your hand felt so good on my head, and I was thinking if papa would only do so, it wouldn't hurt me so much to be sick, and to see poor mamma working all the time so hard."

And the tears rolled one after another down more than one cheek in that little room — that mockery of "home!"

"What do you want, dear? Tell us what to get for you."

"I want to be well, so I can help my mother!"

Was ever answer so eloquent? Who says the children of the poor are not near to God?

How else could such Christ-like sympathy find its way from heart to lips even of little patient sufferers? And God make that reply the bridge over which this little one's father, and other little ones' fathers, can walk to return from the belt of desolate dissipation to the noble love of honest, earnest manhood.

" I want to be well, so I can help my mother!"

By the power given us under the golden shadow under which we write we will burn that sentence in letters of fire around the rim of the glass that father sends to his lips so often, and open his eyes, never to be closed, to the tear-wet prayer of his child —

" I want to be well, so I can help my mother!"

"Well, dear, *you shall* soon be well. And your mother is already helped. Your love helps her. Now tell us what you want beside."

"Shall I tell you just what I want?"

"Yes, just what you want."

" I want some lemonade, for it will taste *so good!* Can I have some ? "

" Why, God love you, little one — you shall have all you want — enough to swim in." .

" When ? "

" When? Right away — soon as we can get it. "

" And may I have an orange, too, sir ? "

" Yes — a dozen of them."

.   .   .   .

She drank of the lemonade, ate an orange — a great big luscious one — and after we had bathed her face, and neck, and little hands and arms with a sponge, wet with Cologne water, she lifted her face a little, put her lips to ours, her arms about our neck, and whispered : —

"*I do thank you, sir!*"

We have heard the wildest, grandest thunder of Heaven, while sitting out in the storm to enjoy the terrific grandeur of the burst, the rumble and the flash which seemed to dance its zig-zag waltz on our very eyelids — we have heard the thunders of brass and steel-mouthed artillery — have heard the death-shrieks of those suddenly called to their final account; but that simple whispered " *I thank you, sir*," from the lips of that father-neglected little sufferer, rises high above the storm, the thunder, the shriek, and is heard even now as we write this simple chapter of fact without effort or attempt to polish, adorn, or beautify.

It cost but little to make her happy. A few kind words. A little money saved from foolish extravagance that we might do good therewith when came the chance and demand. We might have bought a bottle of wine, or treated half a dozen boon companions, and thus helped win fathers and husbands from their love of home; but there would have been no pleasure in that, and not one bit of good accomplished.

And we think of this little patient sufferer — of the thousands all over the land — we can

but feel thankful that we have manhood enough
to take care of our strength, and care for those
we love. There are women all over the land
—women who have homes, little ones they
may be, but homes, and playful children, and
loving husbands. Yet they are not contented,
though a million times better off than many.
There are little children and big ones, dissatis-
fied with what they have, when they are kings
and queens compared to poor little Annie, who
never utters a word of complaint.

And there are men who once loved, and car-
ressed, and cared for their home ones — who
even now are good and kind at heart — who do
not know how their home ones love them, and
pray for them, and long for their sober, loving,
protecting presence — who are too good to
throw themselves away, and leave those who
love them to the chance care of strangers.

And so, little ones, who read this true story
of a little crippled girl — think if you are not

better off than she. You have a home — loving father and mother — some one to love, and to love you — and no drunken father to rob you of pennies, as little Annie's father robs her of the money she earns by sweeping the streets on rainy days, that the rich who cross may not soil their silks or their boots. And when you see poor little children, use them well, and be kind to them, and share your good things with them. Then they will love you, and you all will be better.

And you, good woman, when tempted to scold and find fault with your lot, think if you are not better off than the woman of whom we write.

And you, our brothers — for we all are brothers, after all — look at your family, and thank God that you have manhood, and the strength to care for your loved ones, as they will care for you when comes the time. And when you see a weak brother struggling to rise, help him. Stand by him. Encourage him. Give him employment — at least, kind words, and then we will all of us be better and happier when the work of the week — the battle of life be ended, and we can rest from labor, thanking God for such rest, and for the blessings which follow the good resolves of Saturday Night.

CHAPTER X.

WHY SHE DIED.

THIS Saturday Night the clouds hung dark and heavy over the sun, as at times they will over the stoutest heart. Drops of rain came pattering, then blindly driving against pane and ledge. Then came a wild, shrill, whistling dirge — the clouds lifted and rolled away to reveal the stars and the blue — the Heaven and our Angel watchers.

Storms do not last alway. Herein is hope for all. Many a bright ray — many a gentle breeze — many a cooling whisper of the winds before will come another ending of the week, so we will labor contentedly, and enjoy the beautiful when it comes.

.   .   .   .

To-night as we sat to write there came to us a strange crowd of faces and forms from the beautiful Eternal. Faces we have known — the face of our Guardian Power, with others. The blue of the picture above us is filled with them, and they will speak, so we listen. . . . . . .   A form bear they with them. . . . A heart-wrecked, pale, hungry-souled sufferer. . . .   The face is pale but at rest. . . . Yes, we did know her this side the Great River. We shall know her over there with others who are purified by such agonized suffering as the world little recks of. . . . .

. . .   She is telling us her story — the history of a life. The poison marks are upon her lips, for thus she took her life in her hand and reached its load of blistering agony back to God. . . .   We will tell you as she told us

—as she whispered it to us this night from over there. . . .

"Years ago — O, so many, for the road has been *long* — years ago, when I was a young, trusting, innocent girl — a child in knowledge, he came. He sought me out to ripen his love on my young charms. He came with such low-toned, earnest words, I loved him. I believed in him. His was a haughty, imperious nature, so they told me — a temple of honor. I feared and loved him. It was a strange charm he threw over me — not so much over my heart as my senses. He blinded me with promises. The fires of love, as I thought, burned so deeply in his eyes that I read the road to happiness by the wondrous light thereof.

"He covered me with gifts. He came with love-tokens. He bought me keepsakes.

"He stole me from myself, and buried me under fancied obligations.

"He knelt before me — he plead with me

till my heart gave way, and to his ardent wooing I answered 'Yes.' Then we were married. They said God joined us together! O,
strange, unnatural mating! I became his — he
said I was all his! Then I was happy. One
by one the old friends went their way to other
loves. Avenue after avenue — source after
source of that which gave life, interest, and
pure enjoyment, he closed, lest I might wander from him. . . . Was he afraid of me?

"Afraid to trust one who before God had
vowed love, constancy, and fidelity? . . .
Not all at once, but little by little. Here he
shut a gate. There he erected a wall. Over
there a hedge. And thus he turned me from
the old scenes, the old friends, the old memories. He said I was his! He said our home
was his. He said I might some time be
tempted — he took from me my confidence —
he drank in all my soul — he carried me each
day in his hard, hot, closed hand, and only

opened it when he wanted to toy with me to rest his fancy or cool his blood.

.   .   .   .

" But he was a noble man — the world said. He was not a drunkard — he was not a coarse, profane, vulgar man, careless of rights or opinions of others. He attended church — he wore good clothes — he went in good society, so-called. He took me to his home. It was a little palace. He put carpets under my feet. Books on the tables and shelves. Pictures on the walls. He pointed to the doors and told me to breathe fresh air! He pointed to windows and told me to look out and learn wisdom! He pointed to the couch whereon we slept and told me to await his coming — to fold him to my embrace as was my duty. I obeyed in all things, for I had promised.

" When others were by, he smiled, and talked, and joked, and boasted, and looked wise. He praised me before others, and I

smiled. He dressed me in the best, as he did
his horse. He fed me, as he did his dog. He
gave me work to do — it was done. He bade
me entertain his friends — of mine own I had
none, except with the long agone. Others
said I was happy! . . .

"But when we were alone! His words were
cold, heartless. He was master — I was slave.
He commanded — I obeyed. His words were
cold — his manner heartless — his blood hot —
his delicacy of thought, of touch, of expression, of care was blunted, deadened, poisoned
by those whose embrace gave him excitement.
But the world said I was a happy wife!

"My children learned to fear him. They read
my heart, but I did not wish them to. They
shrank from his coming. They came to me
and wept. Then he was master and tyrant.
The kind hours he once gave me went, never
more to return. I had none to go to — not one.
He withdrew me from others to feast on me

at leisure. His words often and often, and often were cruel, bitter, biting, heart-wounding words. But he cared not. Perhaps I was not perfect. I could have learned from him, but he would not be my teacher. When I was sick he was brutal. He came to me at night, and drank in of my electricity, till all the life I had was gone and on it he grew strong. He mixed with crowds till his vital energies cried for succor, then came to me, absorbed all I had and stood with renewed power over my prostration !

And this was my life. Not a desire in common ! Not a wish born of united hearts ! Not such a life as he had promised, or I had pictured. In fact, it was not a life, but a great, destroying, heart-crushing, murdering agony !

"If he had only spoken kindly to me ! If he had only told me to go from him, and seek more congenial nature. If he had only let me die when I was so often sick in heart and

body ! If he had only abused me in company,
and been kind to me when alone, in our home,
in our room — I could have wept with delight,
and worshipped him. But he cared nothing for
me. I was wan and worn.

.   .   .   .

"What was life to me? I saw other homes
happy. I saw other men kind, and good, and
gentle, and high-minded. I saw poor men,
O! so kind to their wives, that I hated the furniture of my home — I grew tired of the mockery of life — I learned the lesson he gave me
and — and — and — yes, I almost hated him!
But I would do no wrong to him. I was true,
if he was not. I hoped to win him back to me.
I hoped to hear his loving words once more.
But then I did not know, as I know now, that
love once flown is gone forever!

"One day, when weary, very, very weary
of life, I longed for death — for that rest which
of itself was heaven. I wept over the buried

happiness of the past. I sighed for the days of long agone, and tried to still my heart as it contemplated the terrible mockery of life which had been my lot. Hope I had none. He who once was all in all to me was nothing — long since outgrown his unsettled love. Perhaps I had made him miserable. Perhaps I had driven him to unkindness. How? When? God might know — I did not! He lived for no purpose other than to be master, and to point to me as *his*.

.   .   .   .

"At last — at last! Weary, O, so weary of life! Tired of waiting for death. Heart-wrecked and weary of feasting on ashes — with a prayer for him I once loved — with a soul-blind influence over me as it came from the shadow of his unkindness, I looked — I swallowed the key which opened the portals of Eternity and shuddered at what I had done!   .   .   .   I slept. And such a sleep! I dreamed

of the hours of childhood — of girlhood — of
wifehood! And I wished — O! so earnestly
wished that he would give me kind words as
once — that he would pity the ruin he had
made — that he would be the lover as of old.
And then I thought of the road over whose
stony track I had walked — of the mockery of
life I had lived — of the terrible past and its
great agonies — and — then a pitying angel
came and kissed the poison from my lips —
held me to her heart — looked upon me with
her tear-wet face as she sorrowed over my
troubles. . . . I was in strange worlds.
For a moment there were tears, then came
smiles, and looks of hope filled with joy. . .
. It seems so strange there are no unkind
words here. Soon I will be stronger than now,
and then I will walk the golden side of the
Beautiful River to welcome those who come
here for rest. And I will hold them to my
heart, even with such tender love as you would

the darling so dear to you, and kiss the poison from their lips and from their heart. . . . But I could not wait till I had told you of this, so they came — all these dear, good, God-hearted spirits, bearing me on their love to speak with you. And to tell you that we who were crushed on earth, but who now rest in the Eternal Garden, are building out a point of re-membrance-land from shore to shorten the journey, and the sooner welcome all who on earth are good, and kind, and loving, and who will rest with those they truly love, when comes to life its Saturday Night."

CHAPTER XI.

THE BEAUTY OF BETTER WORK.

THERE is something proudly, grandly noble in being a workingman. There is to us unspeakable beauty in labor; in being able to trace letters on the pure white paper before us, to put our thoughts in line, and to know that by work we have made words, sentences, paragraphs, articles, papers, books. And to watch others at work.

The shoemaker fashions from leather, with bits of wood and little threads, the shoe which covers and protects the foot of a woman, while his neighbor, turning from the hot fire of the forge to the cold surface of the anvil, with sturdy blows oft and oft repeated, fashions and finishes his work for the foot of a horse. Each are workingmen — each accomplishes something, and the world is the better for their being here.

The pioneer, with gleaming ax, tramps his way into the forest, sends deep the glittering steel into the astonished timber. The birds fly in affright. The echoes of his blows run through the forest aisles, warning the wilderness to stand back before the triumphs of labor. The tree falls. Its limbs are cut away from the trunk. Looking up, its fall left a little opening, through which we see the blue sky beyond. Again does the ax cut its way — another tree falls — a cabin is lifted into shape — an opening is made in the forest, a home is established there — in time there is a farm, a pretty house, with happy hearts to gather by the hearth and fender — and that man has been of use to the world. God bless him — he is a worker.

The plowman follows the opening furrow day after day till seed-time has gone — then he reaps the reward of his toil, and beholds the golden grain which comes from the soil, the air, the rain, the light, the heat, to repay his efforts, and tell him how glorious it is to labor and to achieve. That man is a worker, a benefactor.

Over there is a poor boy. Coarse his garb — earnest his eye, intelligent his face. Just now he is an apprentice. Day after day he works over the scraps of iron — over the forge — the lathe, the vise. He uses the file and the hammer. His eye reaches farther and farther into the hidden mysteries of science, till at last he is a mechanic, well skilled in his trade. See him now at work. The boy has gone — the earnest man is before us. He is at work, directing others, imparting knowledge, helping to create. A beautiful engine or piece of machinery is before him. It is his work — created out of material other workmen had finished in their line. Proud should our nation be to call such men her children.

There is a glory in work when by it we can achieve success or win the prize of honorable reward. No matter whether that work be in the mine or the forest, on the water or the land, in the pulpit or the sanctum, in teaching, or in protecting interests, hearts, or innocence.

There is a man who is a worker. He loves a girl. He is all care, love, attention, and politeness. He is to her what God is to the Christian — the Hope of Life. And she is to him, if good, and kind, and loving, and in life-harmony with him, a golden-lined pathway, outside of whose sacred boundaries he cannot, he will not walk. Witness the glorious record this worker is making. He builds around a home — he builds within one. He weeds his acts and thoughts and words as a careful man does his garden. He cuts down and pulls up the rough, the thorny, the rank-growing and beauty-killing weeds — he keeps back the cross words, the rough, coarse, vulgar, profane expressions, till no more do this troop of devils-down seek admission to his heart, for it is each day more and more filled with the good, the pure, the loving. He works to subdue himself from the wilderness of nature once so beautiful, now so weed-grown, and become a good, loving, loved, useful man.

His work brings success. His home is each day more attractive. His darling grows into his heart as fragrance into the rose before us, placed there by loving hands, that the eye, when raised from the paper, might rest on the beautiful. He feels a pride, a strength, a glorious heart-rest, which those who are not earnest heart-workers never know. Ours is not a world of chance. It is the result of plan and labor.

If we live but chance lives, we float, sink, and are lost. If we strive to be men, we can all succeed. If we neglect our work, be it to govern ourselves, to make others happier, or to bring form and power out of elements, we but leave the bucket with water to quench our thirst half way up the well, to fall back when we let go.

Thousands upon thousands of men who are now unhappy, might be contented and full of heart-rest, if they would only work. Not alone to build houses but to soften hearts. To help the poor. To make others happy. We love the workers — for they point to their work when comes the nightfall, and truth says they lived to a purpose.

If we work to beautify our hearts, to keep them rightly attuned — preserve our manhood — others will follow our example when they know how happy such work makes the man, the woman, or the child, and we shall thus become such perfect workmen that, in the beautiful Land of the Leal, we shall rest not in mind, but in heart, and be with the near and dear ones all the Eternal Day which follows the soon-coming Saturday Night.

CHAPTER XII.

THE LIGHT ON THE SHORE.

ERHAPS an hour has passed since we bade the widow and three little, fatherless mourners "Good-bye," and then walked slowly homeward, thinking of those we love; of the beautiful flowers kind hands to-day so nicely arranged on our desk; of the weeping, starving mother who this morning called to see if we could not influence a pardon for an erring child in prison — of the home of poverty we visited this afternoon — of the funeral we attended — of the past and the present of one who mourned, and of the happiness which is ours to know that we have such true, loving, earnest, heaven-lit eyes to smile upon us — such good friends to sustain us, and such a glorious work as is ours to be engaged in.

And though it is Saturday Night — though all the week we have worked each day from morn till midnight — though we are very weary, we are happy to know that during all the years of strife, toil, and bitter trials, we have preserved our manhood and saved our strength for good.

Perhaps before comes another Saturday Night we may be called to our rest here and our work there. O! will it not be glorious to *go home,* and be with the loved watchers and the ones who so often and often led us into that wondrously beautiful future, where every flower is more fragrant than the rose, and every act, thought, and deed born of that golden, mellow, hallowed love, which kindles continually the glory of the Eternal!

Soon we will come, golden-haired watchers and waiters who so often troop down to the brink of the river we are sometimes so near across, and then we will rest and listen to the continuation of the wondrous chapters you are so kind as to tell us when others little dream where our thoughts are resting or mind roaming. . . .

To-night we have been almost Over the River. We have seen a few cross safely to the golden sands, but he whom we buried to-day was not with those *we know* await our coming, and who so often smile on us by day and by night. We looked for him, but he was not there. We asked if such an one had passed that way. And they who line the other bank shook their heads and said they were looking not for him, but for the ones he left to mourn — for the broken-hearted mother and the three little ones he had left to test the bitter charity of the world and to starve in neglect.

.   .   .   .

He died Thursday night. We buried him
to-day. Once he was our playmate. Once
with him we built castles in the air and roamed
the hills together. Long, weary, heart-marked
years ago. He was richer than we in boyhood.
He had friends who were wealthy, and could do
as he pleased. He was a favorite at parties
where we could not enter. He was gay, light-
hearted, attractive. But sometimes we thought
him selfish; too proud and overbearing — too
careless of the feelings of others.

One day he told us not to be so familiar in
chatting with a girl, for he loved her. And
she such a sensitive, delicate little thing. We
looked at him with wide-opened eyes. He
simply, yet authoritatively said " Yes," and that
was law. What could weakness do against
strength when the heart was dumb, numb, and
so wondrously quiet? Answer, you who can.

.   .   .   .

One day, sitting in the shade, we saw tears in her eyes. She rested her hand in the one that now guides the pen to this writing, and looked into our face with a waiting look, as do those who now watch all about us. We were tempted to tell her something, when a step was heard — a voice called her — she arose and left us. Her hand has not been in ours since.

. . . One day they were married. It seems but yester eve. But since yester eve all those lines where grief is encamped could not have gathered, so we know it was years ago! She asked us to her wedding, but we had not time to go. The minister pronounced them man and wife.

Then he ordered the wine, and he joked with those assembled. And he drank the health of each guest, and of his bride, and to his absent friends. And he ordered the servants to do this and that. And he ordered a carriage — he ordered her to get ready to ride — he ordered her to tell them good-by — and he ordered the driver to go ahead.

.   .   .   .

One day she came to us — but who would have known her? How years do mark the faces of those whose hearts are bruised! He had lost all. Dissipation had ruined him. For years he had come and gone with scarce a thought of others than himself. His pleasure. His enjoyment. His life. His power. His selfishness. The little ones who came — the little patches of sunshine which came to brighten her home, feared and knew not what it was to love him. When he came they were silent; when he commanded she obeyed. Men said he was coarse, vulgar, profane, selfish, intolerant and unforgiven. But perhaps they did not know. She never said so.

When weary he would go home to rest. When drunk he would go home to become sober. And he used to curse her and called himself a man !

When he left his better self his friends left too. As they always will do. Fortune closed her hand, so he could no more draw flowers from her grasp. The lines on her face — the grief to her heart — the dead look to her eye, did come, but no word of complaint; for the heart of a true woman is proud as her grief is sacred.

We found him sick — without friends — without money — without love, except that unhallowed kind which is born of duty alone. Home of his own he had none — it was long since gone. We found him a wreck. For years he had only looked into the wine-cup — not into the future. And now, when we found him he could not, dared not, look beyond the clouds before him.

Once — years ago, we almost hated him. But not now. Once he seemed to pity us because we were weak. We pitied him now, for he needed it.

One night — after the watch before us beside a vial of medicine marked the hour of two, we sat looking into the future, when he turned, and our eyes met. How glances will run into the past as a keen blade thrusting deeply! He looked at the blankets on the floor where she and they slept, in want, poverty and weariness. Then the tears came to his eyes, as he reached a little way out from the coarse sheet which partly covered him. Hand in hand, our hearts dropped back into the fog of the past, beyond its darkness, and into the sunshine of early life, when, he said, in tones so low, so heart-wretched in utterance : —

" Mark — we were boys years ago. I was the stronger then. Look at me now. Very soon — yes, *very soon* — and it will all be over. But there is no light on yonder shore for me ! I am lost — lost in the fog, as once you remember I was in the woods. *She* who sleeps yonder, I won, took by force, for I wanted none else to have her. She has been good to me — too good for one who — who — who lived for himself alone. —— It is hard to go now —— to leave —— her and them to —— to poverty —— to want —— to distress —— to the care of strangers, when I, who was a man — have not left even a penny or —— a good name for their support. —— Won't you —— for their sake, be good to them, and —— and help them sometimes?" . . .

And very soon he went. Out on the waves. Out in the darkness. Out over bitter and troubled waters. Out in search of the shore where no light beamed for him, for so he told us; and if he did not know, who should? The cries and plaints of those he left behind will not call him back, for they will be cared for, even as we promised him under the seal of death!

.   .   .   .

And now, golden-haired watchers, and warm-hearted welcomers on the Eternal shore, will ye not go up and down till ye find him? He is there, somewhere, for he has gone from us here. Perhaps he has not yet reached you, for the sea is wide to those who have no light on yonder shore, who bear such heavy loads, and who do not know the way as we do. But he will come when his load is washed away. Ye will know him. A man once so stout — so manly — so vigorous — so strong when we were weak; as we were till you threw your wondrous light and golden shadows so full upon us and across our path. Ye will know him by his dissipation-marked face — by his haggard look — by his worn-out nerves — by his bankruptcy!

Find him, if ye can, and care for him, till some day or hour of Eternity, when those who reach the shore, and the light in the East which so welcomes, shall have journeyed far into the interior, he may be able to follow after.

And good friends Over There, if ye cannot find him will ye not throw your light into the hearts of many — O! so many of our brothers, as ye have in ours, that they may see and know the way? And will ye not breathe gentle rest and buoyant hope into the hearts of all the weary wives and neglected children of the land — into the hearts of all who are orphaned and left on the desert coast of a drunken memory, lest they too be lost? And good friends who so smile upon us each day, will ye not fill with kind thoughts all who would be better, that there may be a light on yonder shore when shall come to us all who are here waiting our looked-for *Saturday Night?*

CHAPTER XIII.

BACK TO HER HOME.

DO you remember about the poor woman who came to our office some months ago, pleading with tear-wet face for somebody to help find her daughter who had come to this city to lose herself in the whirlpool of dissipation? We wrote about her bringing a skeleton — the sorrow of her heart — to our sanctum. And her story was this : —

Her daughter had left the parental roof. Without a chart or compass — she had come to New York to follow a life of recklessness. The poor mother mourned for her darling. She brought us her picture — she told her age, her size, her peculiarities of features, and conversation, and, after we promised to find the wandering one, she returned with tear-wet face and grief-laden heart to her vine-clad cottage in a distant town.

We were to write to her mother if we succeeded. Days ran into weeks — weeks into months. We asked the chief of a detective department to aid us. No tidings of the lost one.

One day, in the workshops on Blackwell's Island, where six hundred once innocent but then miserable girls were serving out their sentence, we saw a face like that of the photograph left with us. There could be no mistake. The golden curls were gone, but the face and the eyes were unmistakable. The officers of the prison gave us permission to speak with her.

" What is your name ? "

" Ella Morgan ! "

"No — your other name — the one your mother gave you?"

"None of your business!"

"Come to the window, put your hand in that one; then look us in the face."

"I obey, for I am a prisoner — you wish to humiliate me before all these wretched people."

"Come to the private office for a few moments!"

Downstairs we went to a quiet little prison-like room.

"Now Ella Morgan — look us in the face and see if we came to humiliate you. We know your name now — the prison register tells us. But your name then! When you lived in a vine-clad cottage in the country. When you kissed your mother, and made her happy. Your name before you left home one Tuesday afternoon by a train for this city. Your name when it was —— —— !"

"O! for the love of God — don't speak it aloud! Don't whisper it even. You know all — who are you — what do you want — why are you here — what have I done? Tell me — O! tell me, and pity me — kill me — anything, but don't speak that other name! If you do so others will hear, I'll die. O! sir, don't! For the love of God! don't!"

"Look us in the face — never mind the tears. We do know all. Your mother came to us — she wept like a child for you — her poor heart is broken — she is dying in her home out yonder for the loss of her only darling. She wants you to come back to her — she will never ask where you have been!"

"O, sir, I can not go back! Anywhere but there! To prison — to torture — to ruin — to death! But I can not — I *will not* go home, to be a by-word — to see my mother die — to know that I have brought this sorrow on her, as it is in tenfold weight upon me! No!

Let me live where I am lost — lost — un-known! O, good sir, please do this — and I'll be your *slave!* I'll work for you — *steal for you!* I'll be anything you ask — do any-thing you ask — find a resting-place in the deepest dens of sin, if you will only not tell my mother — not force me to go back to her! I can not again look in her good face!"

"Clara! look here; place your palm on mine; never mind the tears. Now tell us, have you one true, loving friend in all the world who knows you only as Ella Morgan?"

"No; not one!"

"How long since you came here?"

"Twenty-five days."

"How long to stay?"

"Thirty days in all."

"Well, you will stay them here. And then your clothes will be given back to you, in place of that coarse garment of serge. You will come to see us. Come with a gentleman

" Down stairs we went, to a quiet little prison-like room."—*See page* 142

we will send for you. Come in a carriage,
with the windows up, so no one will see you to
annoy. You come to us, *sure*. YOU WILL
COME. This is no place for *you!* You have
suffered enough — your future will be brighter.
Where are your things — your clothes, etc?"

"At No. — West Twenty-sixth street."

"Were you there when arrested?"

"Yes, sir."

"What for?"

"They said I stole a man's watch while he
was drunk in the parlor, but I did not. Some
one did, and put it in my pocket — I did not,
so help me God!"

"Well — we never would arrest any one for
stealing in such places. Let those who go
there to reap take their own chances. But
give us an order for all your things — we will
have them where you will find them when you
come."

"But — but I don't want to!"

10

"Yes, you do — give us the order. And you will come. *Somebody* wants to see you. *Somebody* will be happier than ever before in her life. You will come — and come gladly — to the dearest friend on earth — one who loves you — who will ask nothing of your visit here ! "

"Yes — I'll come — in four days more besides this."

" We'll await you. And now, ——, not Clara — good-by — God save you. Throw the past behind you — be brave for the present — live for the one who *best loves you* for the future — come in four days — till then, good-by.

.   .   .   .

Yesterday afternoon she came, without her prison garb, so unlike the poor girl we saw there. The middle-aged woman, who for an hour had been sitting, standing, crying, laughing, walking the floor, never at rest, was her mother, who came to the city yesterday morning. She wanted to know where we found her darling child. We told her in a large workshop, or manufacturing establishment, on the east side of the city.

We met her at the door. There were two cries of joy. As we passed out upon the street for a few moments, we heard sobs and broken words, but no curses.

A few moments later we found them together — the great tears of joy rolling down their cheeks as both arose to meet us.

.   .   .   .

The poor girl was brave as a heroine of the revolution. She told all — told more than we did. For an hour she sat and talked of the terrible past. She told how she had longed for the world — how she had given herself away, never thinking — how she thought she was smart and able to take care of herself — how she had lived in dissipation; on excitement; drinking wine; submitting herself to that which her soul abhorred for dress, hating herself the while. Then she told of her hours of sorrow — her days of pain and agony — her bitter thoughts — her gradual growing recklessness — her indifference to all save having a revel, and an hour of hilarious dissipation, which would bring sleep to drown thought, till every voice of our heart prayed —

"God pity the unfortunate and give them to some keeping of earnest love rather than this living hell!"

The two wept, and wept. And they laughed and seemed so happy in being together.

A few hours since they left the city, and two happier women we never saw. The mother sold her little cottage and the two will find a home elsewhere. The poor girl left her ill-gotten wardrobe, left all save the keepsakes she brought from home, for she could never again look upon the purchases made at such a fearful price.

Fast as steam can drive, the cars which bear them are going swiftly away. The skeleton the mother brought us months ago is now clothed in love and once more perfect, for that great Power which cares for us as we care for ourselves, has spoken peace to the troubled heart, and she walks to her salvation. We pray God to keep them — to care for them. And may the secret of her visit never be revealed to bring her sorrow. Would to God all people had more charity for those who fall — more heart to help them up — more kind words for the erring.

Happy days are in store for that young girl. She has sickened of her life on ruin's road. Somebody loves her, and will not ask of the past, but will give to her an earnest heart — a true love — a kind, loving home and that *heart-rest* she never knew while living against her womanhood — against nature. It is not what we *have been* but what *we are* that makes us good or bad. And what we will be need not worry us if we labor for the right all the days of the week — guided by our hearts and by our loves through the days of life unto the last and the welcome Saturday Night.

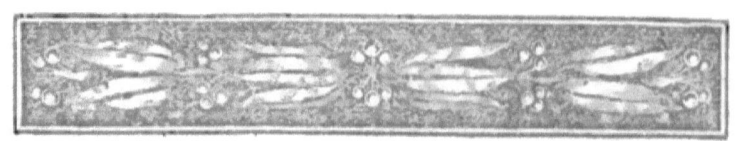

CHAPTER XIV.

DYING AS WE WRITE.

THIS Saturday Night is one of storm, of rude fitful gusts — of dancing leaves — sharp, hurricane whistling, and we are very weary. All the week we have worked more industriously than ever before, for there is so much to do! Not till long after twelve each night have we sought our resting-place to gather strength for the morrow.

And not even one little bit do we feel like writing to-night, for we are sad and weary. Weary from overwork. Sad from what we have seen.

This afternoon we saw two policemen with a drunken woman in a handcart. One was

drawing, the other pushing.   Crowds followed
to gloat their eyes over misery.

"Who have you?"

"One of them!"

"What is the matter?"

"Only drunk."

"Going to the station?"

"No — we are taking her home."

"Where was she?"

"Don't ask so many questions!   Come with
us and I'll tell you all about her.   She went
down to Houston street and got on a breeze —
was upset out in the alley, drunk, and we are
taking her home."

.   .   .   .

Into a by-street — upstairs to a room with
shattered shutters — a patch of carpet — a bed
— a cheap wash-stand — a scratched bureau —
an old trunk in a corner — a little cupboard
over the mantel wherein were a few bottles,
some cold corn beef, a bottle of ale, two cigars,

a greasy pack of cards, and a few little articles of head-dress.

The occupants of the other rooms stared at us as the insensible woman was carried to the third story to the room above spoken of, which an old dame said was hers. Two women disrobed her while we looked about the premises. They laid her on the coarse bed, and called our attention to great bruises over the ribs — over the stomach — a long, dark bruise across the back, where some one must have struck her a fearful blow. And a dark, greenish black spot, half the size of our hand, just under the left breast, told us she had been kicked there by some one terribly in anger.

Very soon one of the policemen returned with a physician, and then they both went away to see who had done all this. The aged, white-haired physician with care examined her — shook his head.

"Badly injured, doctor?"

"Yes — internally.   She cannot live long. Somebody has nearly killed her."

"Under the influence of liquor?"

"Yes — she has been drinking very hard."

And the poor girl, or rather a woman of about twenty-one or two years, lay there breathing heavily.

Her dark hair hung disheveled from a clear-cut brow.   Her eyes were closed — her lips set as if in pain — her heaving, bruised bosom giving evidence of suffering.   She did not look like a bad or vicious girl.   *Only unfortunate!*

Her name was Clara — so the landlady said. She paid three dollars a week for the use of the room.   She came and she went, alone or with company, and no one knew when, where from, or who was with her.   For such is the fashion in places where no one cares what becomes of another.   From other rooms came sounds of mirth and echoes of fearful profanity, as women in half dress or tawdry finery joked with coming or departing guests, **or** swore at each other. To hear such words, such slang, such thieves' jargon, such vulgar, profane, indecent words from woman's lips made us sad. It made us look for a moment on all women as bad, yet *we know* they are not. Only when a woman falls, she falls lower, and soon becomes more disgusting in her misery and her sin than man, for she gives herself wholly to her abandon. Because she has loved — has lost — society scourges her with hot words and lash of devilism, just as society takes fiendish delight in torturing the weak !

And she, poor drunken, murdered Clara, is dying. God pity her more than man does. We do not know who she was, or what her history. But she is a woman. She would be beautiful when dressed, but in all her wardrobe was nothing beautiful. There was a little hat with a red feather. A light white cloak or jacket. Some ribbons stitched on an old dress, and she was ready for the street — for a life sinful, hazardous, awful, terrible — but yet *her life* — all there was of it left to her.

O! merciful Power! O! Great One above us all! Pity, O! pity those who *thus live their life*, and drink the bitter dregs thrown into their cup by hot-blooded, heartless, cruel, reckless humanity.

We have seen her in her pain, her agony, her sorrow, her death; as we have written this simple fact chapter. Dying! Murdered by scores of murderers! By the one who first struck her down! By the parents who did not guard her properly. By the society and Christianity which drove her forth, kicked her in the face, branded her as with a hot stamping-iron, seared her soul and tossed her with curses, gibes, jeers, and devilish malignity, into the living Potter's Field to which those who would escape therefrom are driven back, and back, and back! to their dregs, to their death — to their God's-pity!

Who she was we know not. We never saw her before. Where was she from? Why came she here? Was she lured from her home and its protections? Was she poisoned by flattery, love of dress, and vain show, the glances of men, the remarks on her pretty face, hands, feet, or form? Was she bedeviled by seductive arts and man's higher electrical powers till her soul fell — till she knew not, saw not, cared not for the consequences of the one fatal yielding? Or was she driven out from home by the cold, cruel, harsh, unfeeling, heart-crushing treatment so many men and women give their children by the hearth and fender, all the while thinking it parental duty to harden rather than soften the heart and mellow the life?

She was *somebody's* daughter. Perhaps somebody's sister. May be somebody's betrothed. But now, O God! pity her — take her — keep her — renew her purity in the Land of the Leal by Thy wonderful alchemy, and give her there the· friends, the life, the happiness not hers to enjoy on earth.

Once she was good and pure. Her infant hands rested on the face of a father — the bosom of a mother. Her little smile gave joy. Her little lips kissed as sweetly as do the lips of thousands whose fathers and mothers will read this chapter. Once she nestled in the arms, and in the heart of somebody. Little did that somebody know she was to die thus, or they had rather she had died in her innocent infancy.

Perhaps she was to blame for this sorrow to some extent. But not all. Perhaps her mother, her father, never tried to teach her. Then they are guilty of her murder. Perhaps her father was cross, cold, ugly, dissipated, and neglectful of his duty as a man, and as a parent.

Thus teaching her that home was not a place for happiness. Perhaps he disgusted her young life, and thereby planted seeds for the weeds that grow in shame over the grave of the unfortunate. Perhaps he was coarse, rough, brutal, unfeeling, and thus drove her forth to wander in bitterness.

Perhaps he himself died a poor victim to dissipation and threw his loved ones upon a cruel world, not to be supported, but tempted, tossed, trampled upon, and driven to anything for that life which, but for the love we all have of life, had better be lost! How many thousands of loving ones have been thrown into temptations from cold, unfeeling homes, where cross words, bitter words, unloving words; bare floors, bare walls, and lack of comfort have steeled the heart and fitted it to risk any chance rather than endure torture!

But she is dying. Poor, bruised, heart-wrecked, murdered one! Some may say,

"Good enough for her!" *For shame!* Are hearts thus cruel born of God or devils?

Look upon your loved ones and tell us if you would curse them, should they fall by the way when too weak to walk! And see if you cannot save your own, and help save others. If they fall help them up again and be kind to them. Pity, but do not condemn, for it may be you will condemn the one who is not to blame! And then who will be the most guilty?

. . . .

Soon they will bear her away. No one will weep over her grave. A cheap funeral. No one will wonder where she is — why she comes not. She will not be seen on the streets with that wild, hunted, horror look — but some one else will take her place. The little room will be let for three dollars a week to some one else. The bed where is dying the bruised girl will soon be cleared of its burden — the sheets spread smoothly — her little keepsakes overhauled and thrown away, and no one will miss her.

God love those who are good — and those who are striving to do right — who are true, and kind, and loving to each other. Let us forgive and forget the little spots of the past, as God will forgive us all our life-blotches. Let us do anything rather than drive the heart-wrecked ones to death, or to that dissipation in unloving recklessness which leads thereto.

Then come, loved one, closer and *still closer* to the lips, the love, the arms which will protect thee, and the heart which loves, and so let all our hearts and lives be filled with such goodness and charity, as will make us who are but mortals not forget that others are mortal; tempted and unprotected, not strong. For if we have not charity, how will others have tears or charity for us when comes to earthly life its rest and final Saturday Night?

11

CHAPTER XV.

HOME, AND WHY IT IS HOME.

E built a castle in the air! All the years of our life were we building it. Some there were who laughed at us; but what of that? Let those laugh who win. And so to-night, as we sit by the table in our little home, not man nor monarch is half so happy as we.

Years ago, when the heart was hopeful, we looked ahead to the time when we might have a happy home, and beautiful works of art therein on which to rest the eye, as the beautiful queen of the home would rest our heart. But how should we have all this, and when?

By work — whispered the spirit of pluck, and so we learned to labor and to wait. And so we have worked these many years — always contented and hopeful. Content to labor, hoping to enjoy the reward, as do all who are creative, and thus fit to work Over There for the completion of the wondrous revealment.

Ours now is a beautiful home. Here we are happy and content. These walls we helped build. Not that we piled high the brick, iron, stone and marble one above the other, or helped drive the nails. But we worked at something else, and earned to pay for this. And now we are very, very happy, and never a man so stout of heart. Work does not tire us, for we see the result and reward earnest work does bring.

This little place we call home. And the beautiful pictures on the walls all about. The carpet on the floors, so we can walk while our darling sleeps just there — so we can rest our left hand on her brow, and not waken her, for she is weary, perhaps. The chairs, the tables, the sofas, the ottomans, the easy-chairs — the books, musical instruments and all these scores of beautiful things in the room, we earned! They are ours. Honestly ours. Never a man, woman, or child robbed of a single penny for their obtaining.

It is glorious to work. Little by little we have won all these by honest toil. And we have put them together — and here, surrounded by 'what we have earned, and cared for by the one we love, we are happy. And strong to create or to earn more — to help others — to encourage the good — to draw sword, if need be, in defence of virtue, the widow, and the fatherless.

We pity those who have no homes, who have no happy homes, where life passes in love, contentment, and enjoyment of perfect confidence in each other. We pity those whose lives are wasting away in dissipation, till they will enter the Eternal so wasted and unimproved that they will be but specks on the floors, so to speak. And we pity all who are not happy — who are not mated and in unison of feeling one with the other — who do not feel it a joy to live for and with each other; for, after all, this is the true life, which is but the germ of Love Eternal. For those who cannot love each other here and have sympathy with all, are not guided aright.

     .   .   .   .

It is very still out-of-doors to-night. It is near midnight, still our work is not quite done. That is, we cannot sleep yet, nor can we bear to waken the dear one who slumbers just beside us. So we let her rest. She has been such a help to us. Has cared for us so kindly and with such tenderness, as Mary cared for Him she so loved while He was on earth. When we are sick and prostrate from overwork, how like a ray of light from Over There does she come with careful whispers, gentle touch, sweet breath and absorbing solicitude to watch over and care for us!

How carefully she closes the blinds and draws the curtains to exclude the light while we sleep! How well does she remember the most minute item of instructions given by the good physician, who also comes to lend his aid and skill!

And when the pain blinds our eyes, and nearly sets us wild, how her soft fingers, gently passing over throbbing temples and fever-heated brow, will quiet the little devils in the burning blood, and teach them obedience to her will! It is she who opens and closes the door so noiselessly, and makes herself again our saviour for the continuation of the work we know it is our duty to perform here to be fitted for Over There.

Yes, this is our home. And she is our

darling. Perhaps you do not like her; we do. Perhaps you love her. Not so well as we do. You may think her beautiful. So she is; but to one who has studied life, there is no beauty like that of her pure mind and God-given intellect. You may not think her beautiful. You do not know her — her pure life — her confiding love — her sympathy and generous willingness to aid us in all that will make others happy or alleviate suffering. You do not know how happy she makes our home — how she cares while we labor; how she believes in us and thus puts it upon our honor to be good and true; how her heart goes out to those who are needy, in distress, unfortunate.

She is sleeping now. Never a babe sleeping more sweetly. A smile on her face even yet — this hour and more there resting, as the hand, so soft, so fair, so full of kindness even in its sleeping touch, resting so temptingly where we can reach it in a moment. We know she is happy, and do wish that all the women in the land were as happy as is she. When comes the hour for rest, then come we to our home. This makes it a home. And a man will always be where his heart is, and it is well that it is so. She is not afraid to trust us, and does trust us implicitly. And so trusting, not for all the wealth of the world would we deceive her, for then would her happiness and our happiness be gone, and regretful sorrow be left in its stead.

Who does not love a happy home? Who is there not striving to obtain one? And who does not worship those who make him happy — even as we worship God because He has promised us eternal happiness? And so we love her who is sleeping just here. She is very, very good to us. To all she is ever a lady, never stooping to gossip, to slander, to tattling of her neighbors, never envious, but always so pure, gentle, earnest and womanly that we cannot help writing of her, and stopping now and then to press light kisses on her brow, and to study the face and the life of our darling, but for whom home would not be home — life not be life — happiness not happiness, and words of promise perhaps not so sacredly kept.

And so, while she sleeps so beautiful and so beautifully, we pass this chapter, perhaps the very last we can or ever shall write, into a tribute to home, and to the pure, virtuous, loving, noble, refined women of the land, who do so much to make man and home happy, but who are too often unappreciated sufferers at the hands and hearts of those who have no love for the beauties of home and the love which surrounds and hallows it. May the love and care of our good angels be with all who strive to make home, no matter how humble it may be, happy as is ours this finished Saturday Night.

CHAPTER XVI.

WORKING AND WAITING.

E knew it would come!

The best of all the nights given us to think, to rest, to resolve — the Saturday Night. All we had to do with its coming was to labor earnestly and wait contentedly. All in good time, as 'twas appointed, the good night has come, and now we can enjoy the heart-resting reward it brings, and look at the picture on which we have labored. A week. A picture with seven ideas — each one a day. And so we are all artists.

The week is the canvas. We are the artists. Events are the colors. When comes the beautiful Saturday Night, this one of our pictures is finished, and is taken on the breath of the dying week, to be looked at by Him who is Love and Power, and then hung in the Great Parlor, or out in the Rubbish Room, as the picture is worthy. Each picture will be the simple record of our acts. If they be good and suggestive of the beautiful, they will be given place with other pictures of beauty. If not, they will not be hung where they will mar the scene or detract from other beauties. Over There will be two exhibition rooms — for the good and the bad. And we shall look at our pictures and see wherein we failed or succeeded, for time is the pencil that to the canvas of Eternity our every act transmits.

And so the weeks come and go. Each Saturday night we pause to look at our work before the midnight hour takes from the frame the canvas whereon we have wrought, and a fresh one for the week to come in its place

doth leave! We earnestly try to discover
where we have touched too lightly or too heavily. We try to see if we have in the least
failed to do strict justice with liberal tinting
given to all — for we are none of us perfect.

And let us strive, good friends, that each Saturday Night our work may seem more and
more worthy to be called a picture. These
pictures have many defects. Cross words.
Marks of reckless temper, heated by words of
others, which pain and wound. If we each
week labor more and more for the poor, the
oppressed, the weary-hearted and overtasked,
it seems as if we were drinking deeper of that
pure water which so takes away selfishness and
directs the soul to good deeds and generous
impulses. Those who are on the right road
and nearing a happy home, where loved ones
with outstretched arms await them, feel the
heart grow lighter over the lessening dis-
tance.

And it is so beautiful to have a home — a welcome — a reward of love, to draw you to that rest so few know. Is it not heaven to know that in all its world there is one spot where you can rest — one heart to rest with — one presence, as that of a God, in which you can bask and grow strong for the race and the work of the morrow? To feel that there is one to whom you can go with all your troubles, doubts and fears — one who will listen to you in love, forgive and forgive again, if need be, till manhood, ashamed of its weakness, is purified to strength by love protected. A home on earth to which we can come and find one who will listen to us and lift us up, as He who is so good will listen to us, forgive, and throw about our spirits the golden light of pure life-thoughts, till we shall, by our own earnest efforts and His protecting direction, grow away from that part of our nature which, unchecked and uncontrolled, holds us to the earth and to misery.

As our home Over There will be beautiful, so is our home here, and our work, and our resting. As this Saturday Night has come, so will others, and then we shall rest in happiness. We know it. For it has been told us. And the same one who has so helped us here — so encouraged and rewarded us by kind words and gentle care — will go home with us — we may be separated a little while, but we shall be united, never to part, with no more mortal experiments, living, resting, rewarded for our earnest working and continued constancy here by a never-ending life and labor without weariness in that Land of the Leal whose Alpha and Omega will be Love and Power Eternal.

All this for those who make perfect life-pictures here. Who dare follow the great light hung high in the heavens for all who dare look up and follow, no matter what the crowd may say. All this for those who dare stand erect before man, bowing only before the Holy Presence. Who dare live lives to reach, and walk in paths by higher powers directed, caring nothing for the criticism of those whose work or pictures are no more perfect than our own!

If we live for the speech of men here, we do not live for the Great Reward there, for the criticism of Time has no weight in Eternity, except through the certainty that good deeds will follow us as flowers bloom over graves to mark where rests the face after the smile has gone, and where molds the worn-out tenement of the soul.

All in good time reward will come. The rivulet reaches the ocean after its race be run, not before. It sings on its way and gives joy. It gives life to what it touches, and a home to the beauties which live in its waters. In good time it mixes with the waters of the deep, and the whispered eloquence of the rivulet is mingled in the great prayer to God from the depths of its harmonious life.

To fret, to scold, to worry ourselves and worry others, will not add beauty to the picture. Stopping work at noon will not bring the sunset and the proper hour for rest. Annoying others will not make us happier. Harsh words will not lighten our own hearts. There is more of life than all this. If this person does this, or that person does that, all this is nothing to our eternal effecting, for we are judged and given work to do Over There, not for our meddling, our fault-finding, our interfering with that which does not concern us, but for ability and willingness to govern ourselves and work on our own pictures.

And if our work be well done — if we shall

strive to make only beautiful pictures, happy will we be in enjoying the beautiful rest which will be for all who well and truly work and wait for the final Saturday Night.

CHAPTER XVII.

TRYING TO BE RICH!

AGAIN goes a week with its wondrous freight of good and evil — of joy and sorrow — of life and death, as the wail of the new-born and moan of the dying make the woof and warp of our existence.

And what a checkered life is this at best! And how foolish are we all to so cling to its labors and to dread the coming hour of dissolution and release from earth, which is the prison of the soul.

To-night a boy came to our room. A pale-faced, studious, honest-looking little fellow of twelve years. We were seated at the desk in our private apartment, when there came a timid knock on the door. Doubting whether any one rapped or not, we bade a pleasant entrance, and the little fellow stood before us. . . . Now he has gone out we will tell our little boy friends about our conversation. This boy who called on us to-night was a poor — a very poor boy. He worked in a kindling-wood factory up town. A place where pine cord-wood is sawed into little blocks about six inches long, then split up into sticks about an inch square, tied into little bundles large enough to fill the crown of your hat, and sold to be used in kindling coal fires in grates.

His hands were ever so hard — just as ours were once, years ago, when we were a poor boy working on a farm, husking corn for a quarter of a dollar per day. But these were happy days, for all we were but a poor boy.

They were happy, because we tried our best to make them so.

His little brown linen pants were too short and too small for him, and his shirt, though clean, was coarse and serviceable. But the clothes are nothing. They wear out! In thinking of great men we never stop to wonder how they were dressed — we remember them by their acts.

"Good-evening, my little man. Will you walk in?"

"Yes, sir, if you please. Is this Mr. Pomeroy, who writes every Saturday Night?"

"Yes — come in and be seated. Take the easy-chair, for you look tired."

"Thank you, sir, very much."

"Not at all. What is your name, and what can I do for you?"

"My name is Henry Stephens, and I didn't know but you would talk with me a few moments to-night. I have all summer wanted to come, ever since my mother died. And last night it seemed as if she came to me in my dreams and told me to come to you to-night, and I could not help coming, sir."

"You did right. Now what can I do for you? Perhaps nothing — but we will see — How old are you?"

"Twelve years old, sir."

"Where do you work, and what do you work at, Henry?"

"I pack up kindling for Mr. ——, on Twenty-third street.

"How much do you earn?"

"Four dollars a week, sir."

"And board yourself?"

"I board with my aunt for three dollars a week and washing."

"Where is your father?"

"He died five years ago."

"In the army, or where, and how?"

"He was hurt in a fight on Baxter street, in

a place where men were talking politics, and he died."

" When did your mother die ? "

"Last winter, sir — the 14th of January."

" Was she poor ? "

"Yes, sir; she worked by the day in a laundry."

"Have you much education ? "

"Not much; I can read pretty good, and write and cipher some, and know a little about geography."

"That is good. What do you want me to do for you ? "

"I want you to tell me how to get rich and be good."

"That is easily done, Henry. Poor boys make the richest and the best men, as poor girls generally make the best women. Most all the rich men and the great men in this country were once poor boys. They worked. And you can work. Learn a trade. Learn it well, then stick to it like a man. And try to be the best workman of all. Do not fool away time, for time is money. To build much of a church takes much planning, and more work. If you sit by the roadside on a stone all day, you need not look for it high on the wall at night. And always be careful of yourself, your health and your reputation. Save a part of what you earn — if but a penny a day. Be neat and clean as you can. You need not be a slouch, if you are poor. And, Henry, always keep your temper if you possibly can, for good-natured men have the most friends, and get along the best.

" Try to be able to take charge of the business you are in, and when you do, be careful to advance the interests of your employer. He will respect you then — advance your wages, and do better by you each year, till at last you will become a partner, or have enough money

to start business for yourself.   Work honestly.
Have patience.

"And, Henry, remember this.   Money does
not make us rich.   The richest man of all rich
men in the world is he who does the most
good, and most loves the poor and the unfortunate."

"My health is not very good, sir."

"Then you must take the better care of it,
or your dream of life will never be realized."

"Sometimes I think it never will, and feel
tired of trying."

"We all feel just that way at times.   But
the best way is to get over it, and do the very
best we can.   And all of us can do more than
we do, if we try right hard.   We can try till
we die."

"I don't want to die!"

"Why?"

"Because I want to live and have a home
some day.   And I am afraid to die!"

"*Afraid?*"

"Yes, sir."

"What an idea! Were you afraid to come here to-night to see me?"

"*No, sir.*"

"Why not?"

"Because I read your book, and I knew you would not harm me. And my Sunday-school teacher said I could come to you, and you would talk with me."

"That was right, Henry. You were not afraid to come here. And this is a finer place than your shop, with its saws, knives, and slivers. So our Home in the Land of the Leal, which is called Home or Heaven, is millions of times more beautiful than this. And all can enter who come the right way. And no one there will drive us out. Death is no more than opening the door through which you come from a dimly-lighted hall to a brilliantly-lighted parlor. Out there

it is dark. There are stairs to climb before
you reach here. And a door to open before
you can enter. Are you sorry you came here,
Henry?"

"No, sir — I am glad."

"Well, death is no more than the swinging
of that door. It opens from darkness to light.
And when we die we but just begin to live.
It will take us a long time to know all there is
of Heaven. But there is One there who knows
and we can learn of Him, for, Henry, there is
a God, who is that great loving Power so few
understand aright.

"As we are good, or strive to be good here,
and to do by others as we would have them do
by us, so will we be the happier Over There,
for in the home of disembodied spirits there
will be degrees of happiness as here — work to
do as here — a greater life to live than here.
And there we shall *move* with the multitude as
here, but shall *rest* with those who think

liberally and in whose hearts the beautiful, God-spoken principles of loving forgiveness shall have taken root.

"We never shall be worse off than here. But some will be happier there than here, for they will have more to their credit — will have higher responsibilities, they are being fitted for a grander work. The soul does not die, for it is of the vital principle of Life Eternal. Nor will it ever roast in endless fire, as once men taught who groped blindly in bigotry and superstition.

"There is nothing of death to fear. But for the pain of brief separation from those we love here, we could even now lean back in our chair, rest a hand on the desk, and sleep to awaken in a better place than this, as this is better than a dark, unfurnished hall. We would gladly die, this moment, except that our work is not yet finished, and we would not leave our loved ones so long to the care of others.

"Henry, as a man looks over his workmen to see who of them are the most worthy; who he will have to do this and to do that, so does the Loving Power look us all over to see who He will make rulers over many things in the beautiful Land of the Leal. And if we be not earnest workers here, we shall deeply regret it Over There, where the growth of the soul is less rapid if we have not an experienced life on earth.

"And so, my earnest young friend, be not afraid of death. Better be afraid of life! Here we are making a record to be looked at There. We had better be afraid of ourselves. Remember that money does not make us rich, for There, dollars do not count. Thus we have told you how to be rich and good, as we try to be, and as we hope all the earnest boys and men of the land will be, with no regrets for misspent time when shall come the good, the beautiful rest of Life's final 'Saturday Night.'"

CHAPTER XVIII.

INDEED A GOLDEN REWARD.

WE did hope for a rest this Saturday Night, all alone, with no one to take our thoughts from the beautiful study of life, and visiting with the good angels who come at times trooping all around us, each one suggesting a good thought and all smiling a happy-hearted approval to reward us for honest laboring in the vineyard of life.

Have you ever read of angels' visits? Some people say they are few and far between. Not so, if we would have them frequent. We believe in the visits of angels. Not the looked-for embodiment with wings and white

raiment, which appear to wandering imagina-
tions. But the good angels, whose home is
space — whose resting-place is Over There —
who live in the yellow sunlight of the Eternal,
and whose mission is to welcome There the
ones who lived liberal, noble lives here.

Our good angels never yet have deserted
us. Each year more come — none are missed.
We know many of them. We can see them as
plainly as the tracing on the paper before us.
Sometimes a troop of them come to have silent
talk with us, then away they all go to their
missions. Some of them go on missions of
their own, as beautiful birds fly through the
air — as the spirit — the thought, annihilates
space.

The pathway they go — the way they
come — is not dark to us. It was once. But
we have looked for light and looked and
looked, till at last it has come to us. We
would not stop looking till we saw, and under-

stood. Every day these unseen visitors come to us. They are our friends. Sometimes one, sometimes more are with us. At times they leave us alone, and go away to call upon others. Sometimes we send them on errands for us, miles away — to whisper thoughts to absent friends. And they come back to tell us what their hearts replied, and where they were, how looking, and how in health. So we are a thousand times a day here and there — with those who write us letters — with the poor who often think of us as we do of them — with the weary and the overworked.

Sometimes all our good angels leave us for hours, to grope in the dark, as it were, and to feel sad, depressed, unnatural, as one who halts in a wilderness, with the night and the storm all about him, and he in distress. Then we make haste to call for help, and our spirit reaches forth and goes out for the golden shadows, which brings us light.

And they come. One whispers hope. Another tells us to be brave and truthful, and all will be well. Another tells us that the golden shore is for our reaching, that we must not sit idle, but push on like a man. Another good angel comes and tells us what others have done — another one tells us who loves us and who is glad when we are in such heart-warmed company — other angels go with us to point the way, and show where we must walk and not fall; and once more we are on the road.

Sometimes, when our good thoughts or good angels come to us not, dark shadows come over us. Bad thoughts and desires enter our spirit temple. But light dispels darkness, and the good triumphs over the bad as we seek the light or remain content to grope in darkness, and to sleep under this hedge or that bramble because others who do not, and perhaps do not care to

"A well-dressed man, more than a dozen years our senior, entered." —
See page 191.

see as we see, are content to think there is but one path to the Eternal!

And that one over thorns, and coals, and poisonous points of granite — as if a Power that is Love Eternal wants agony instead of earnest manhood and good-will in the beautiful Land of the Leal.

.   .   .   .

We were hoping to-night that we might visit with our good angels, and tell them how they had helped us all the days of the week, and ask them to leave with us each a good resolve for the week to come. But it was not to be.

There was a pull at the door-bell down stairs. The kind janitor of the building who keeps the door securely tyled when comes nightfall, and we are alone, came and said a gentleman wished to see us on important business.

"What is his name?"

"He did not state, sir, but he said he wanted to see you a little while to-night."

13

"Show him up."

And he came. A well-dressed man more than a dozen years our senior. His step was firm — his face clean and noble — his eye bright. He came forward, and reached out his hand —

"Good evening, good friend."

"Welcome, — will you rest in that easy-chair?"

"Thank you, and excuse me for this interruption. You do not remember me? I am glad of it."

"We have met before. Your eyes are pictured on my memory, but where we have met I cannot tell."

He continued —

"Do you remember seeing a poor drunken man in the depot at Cleveland in 1864 — a man who was kicked like a vagabond dog for stealing an apple?"

"Yes."

" Do you remember following that man to the corner of the depot, outside, by the track, and asking him why he took the apple ? "

" Yes."

" Do you remember that he told you he had eaten no food for two days — that he had been on a drunken spree — had no more money and not a friend to go to, and was starving ? "

" Yes."

" Do you remember bringing a little pie and a sandwich, and of saying a few kind words to that man ? "

" Yes."

" Do you know me, now ? "

" Yes — I know you to be that man, for whom I was sorry."

"Well, sir — I am that man.   And to-night I come to pay you for that pie and that sandwich.   Will you accept this little gold dollar as an evidence of friendship and gratitude ?   I ate the food you gave me — and ate no more

till I *earned it*. The taste of that food was in
my mouth many hours, but it was not so sweet
or so nourishing as the kind words you gave
me, never forgotten."

"I have forgotten them!"

"Well, I have not, and will tell you what
you said, 'Take this lunch and a little courage
—then take care of yourself and help me
sometime.'"

"That was not much to say."

"It was a great deal to me. I looked at
you as I ate, till you got on the cars, and then
I walked away. Your words gave me pluck.
The idea that I could ever help you seemed ri-
diculous. Then I said, why not? I walked
away from there — walked out, away out Eu-
clid avenue, and found a chance to work five
days, helping a man fix a barn. And I didn't
drink any more.

"Then I got work in a warehouse for a
month. Then went to Idaho and made money.

Two years since I saw you in Chicago, and remembered your face. I followed you till I learned who you were. Now my business called me to New York, and I come to tell you that the poor, drunken vagabond to whom you gave a few kind words a few years since is now well off, as the world counts, and that I want you to take this little keepsake and wear it, or give it to some other poor creature."

"I will accept it with pleasure. And keep it as long as I live, to remind me that a kind word costs nothing and often does much good."

"Yes, you gave me food, and courage, and something to think of. I said I would try to be kind to myself if a stranger could be kind to me."

"And you have done well, have you?"

"Yes, first-rate. I kept at work, and saved what I earned. Went West soon as I could, and kept going West. Made a little money at Cheyenne. Then I went to mining and knocking around in Idaho. Sometimes it was pretty blue, but I kept at it, and now I am all right. Some day, when you want a friend, call on me and I will repay you for your kind words, which will never be forgotten."

He went away, and we went to our work, and to the enjoyment of the reward which is ours this beautiful Saturday Night.

CHAPTER XIX.

MERELY OPENING A DOOR!

IN a little church-yard out from the great city, near our olden home, a new-made grave marks a new comer to the city of the dead since last we sat to our Saturday Night writing.

A full-length grave in a country church-yard; just under the shadow of the steeple which rises above the maples — under the tremor of the little bell up there — out from a close, narrow, cramped life into his allotment of labor and reward in the broad lasting Over the River.

We knew him years ago. A brave, fearless

youth. A noble man. There were more
thorns than roses in the garden of his young
life, but he worked well and bravely, heeding
not the brambles, but gathering the roses, till
he plucked many bouquets to gladden hearts
and beautify homes. Narrower than the lonely
chamber of silence in which the form in which
he once lived now reposes were the ideas
taught him in the years agone. But there was
in his soul a desire for light and truth. And
so, the growing wings of intellect beat against
the prison-bars fastened across his mind's
vision, till at last they broke down the dark
barriers of ignorance, and out in the free air,
he rode over the storms to survey the new rest
and the new Home so beautifully called
Heaven.

One day, months ago, when we saw him by
the hearth and fender, sitting beside, and holding on his arm and bosom his loved and beautiful darling, whose clear eye and gentle love

made his life golden, like her hair. We almost envied him the quiet, real life he enjoyed in his little country home. It was so unlike ours — so widely different from the busy, tiresome, endless drudgery of our labor, that we would have given him all we had for the beautiful life he was living — for his sweet home-rest.

We talked long of our lives and what had come to us in the years agone. It was not long ago. We once expected to go first to the other life, for he had better health than we. He drew *so close* to his heart the beautiful darling, all his own — he pressed at times such light yet lasting kisses upon her brow and lips as she rested there watching for the words that came, that we looked again and saw her as in a vision alone — as now. At last we said : —

"You are the nearer home."

" Why think so ? "

"To-night we have seen our messengers,

To us they say, 'Not yet!' all the while closer
and still closer, locking and interlocking the
souls of you two who are so good, kind, and
true to each other. She will soon follow you
to the Land of the Leal, where you shall indeed be as one."

Then her arms drew still closer about his
neck, and he bent low to smooth the golden
hair and to kiss away the tears from the eyes
of her he loved. Ah, good friends — that
simple home of a fellow-laborer was more of a
palace than are many mansions.

Then, when all was still a few moments —
and we were looking out of a window watching
the star we learned years ago to call our own,
after she who rested there so sweetly on the
bosom of a true, earnest, loving, thoughtful
husband, had turned her head so we could not
see her eyes, he said:

"Sometimes I think the day will not be so
long, and I am ready to go — but who will

care for my Darling? This is all that holds me to life after the work I am to do is finished. Who will care for her as I do? Who will hold her life as I do? Who will protect the one for whom I will be waiting, and whose life must be with mine to complete the life of both, Over There?

"You will protect her?"

Then I am ready to go at any time. This was all that held me here. To be sure, it is beautiful here — we all wish to stay, but it will be more beautiful There, and to our new home I am ready to go, and wait for her. Sometimes — yes, often, when from home — I feel a momentary dread of death as I think of old lessons, but the cloud soon floats away, and I see the sky beyond, as now. Tell me of it, and we will both listen."

There is so much to tell! You will know it all before we can tell you. Clouds come, and the eye rests thereon. If you allow your eye to follow and rest on clouds, it will lead your gaze trackless journeys — but if you look only for the Light in the East — for the sky beyond — the cloud will pass away, and you will look upon a reality. So with our lives — if we look steadfastly, and thus do strive, a reward will be ours all in good time.

Death is nothing to be dreaded — no more than the "good-night" parting at the door when we leave a crowded party for the beauty of our home, just a little way through the darkness. We do not fear to sleep, for we shall waken again. And our sleep, resting, and awaking is much as we make it. We can so live and partake during the day that we will have troublous dreams at night and a fever-shaken brain on the morrow. Or we can so live to-day that our rest to-night will be sweet, and to-morrow we will waken refreshed, ready for the work or the journey, as duty calls or inclination leads the way.

"Why not go now?" you may ask. Why does not fruit fall before it is ripe and yet be good? Why does not the babe become a man at once? Why come bud and flower — seedtime and harvest — the ripening of manhood as of grain? It is not all for us alone! This life nor the next are for us in selfishness!

There is work to do there as here, and we shall be called to that work when wanted, and they who begin at the eleventh hour will be rewarded accordingly. We shall be changed from darkness to light, as our bodies are changed from corruption to earth when we are through with them, as tenements no longer fit to live in.

There is no more danger in the night than in the day — the darkness than the light — if we know how to walk and go only in the true light. It is less work to drop a heavy load than to carry it — so it is easier to part with a life well spent than to guard it carefully over dangerous roads. "Come to me all ye who are weary and heavy laden, and I will give you rest."

How beautiful that in the Great Powerful! *All* who are laden! We are to have rest — not agony. And when the time comes, we will go as our friend went. Brave, hopeful, confiding. If we take care of ourselves *here*, He will take care of us *There!*

There are many ways to reach the great work of the future. We may dread to tell those who cannot go just now, "good-bye." It may seem impossible that the walls of the house should part; but when comes the time to go, a door will open — we can pass out and know that we are still safe. Then we will take care not to loiter by the way — and He will care for us.

Thus went our friend — and there shall we find him. And the dear one he left will be cared for till she, too, will be ready to see the door open, and can step forth to light and life eternal, happy in his love there as she was here, if she will be pure and deserving, as all who are of good intent will be or strive to be. But a little while longer, then we, too, can go. It will be hard to part with those we love, but thank God there will be others there to welcome us as we will be ready to welcome the one who is our life and solace here, while working to earn the reward which comes with the Saturday Night.

CHAPTER XX.

THIS Saturday Night we are weary. And who that works is not? Day after day it is work, work, from morn till midnight. We work to gain an influence for good. To see how far ahead we can get from the ignorance common to us all at birth — to the knowledge of the Eternal. To see how we can make others better and happier — to earn comforts for those we love.

If we were Santa Claus!

If we could make such presents as we would like to this night!

208

We would give to Christians more liberty, and thus make all men Christians.

We would give success in life to every earnest worker.

We would give pity to every unfortunate, no matter who.

We would give to all charity, even as Christ Jesus gave charity.

We would give to every person in the world a happy home, and a heart filled only with love.

We would give to all men, virtuous, loving, happy wives; and to all women, true, fearless, loving, careful, considerate, temperate husbands.

We would give all the workingmen of our country happy homes and encouragement. We would like to give presents to all the children who read this paper, or who hear it read to them. But this we can not do. So we

14

write this article for their benefit, and talk to the fathers and mothers.

The new year has begun. We hope it will be happier and more filled with blessings than the last. We hope all the little children gathered by the fireside in city or country homes may live till comes the next New Year, and be very happy all the time! Will fathers and mothers try to make them so?

Not so much by giving presents of toys as of kind words. Not by expenditures they are not able to make, but by showing the little ones the way to be good and happy.

Who of the dear, good mothers who so love their little ones will agree not to speak cross; not to punish when in anger; not to get mad and provoked at little things, which children always do because they are children, and do not know better till they have been taught? Who, of the kind, loving mothers who read this, will resolve to be more and more careful of the hearts of their little ones each day, and to keep them from the storms of words, which darken the sky of young life and so cut in upon the harmony necessary to perfect growth?

You can not grow a beautiful plant to beauty and perfect blossoming by showering it with hot and cold water — by throwing sticks and stones upon it; by pinching, twisting it this way and that; by pulling it up in the morn, to set it back in the earth at night.

No more can you rear a child to love, and goodness, and purity, and harmony of character, by being first cross, then kind, then ugly, then loving, then angered, then in coaxing mood till the young soul be driven from point to point, gaining never a rest or foothold on the beautiful lawn of a loving, harmonious life.

And who of the fathers who read this will be good fathers, and set good examples for their little ones? We wish every father in the land would leave off his rough, vulgar, profane talk. His little ones would love him so much the better and would grow to be better and purer. Children often think more of their mothers than they do of their fathers.

Do you know why this is so? We will tell you. The young mind is pure. It takes to purity naturally. The mother utters fewer hard, coarse, rough words than does the father. The child, budding, growing to manhood, clings to the smoothest, sweetest, most even life, and when come from the father's lips words antagonistic to the pure young soul, it turns to the mother. And if she be cross, and rough, and cold, and uneven, the little one turns to the world, too often to be lost before it can realize that there is another Power to turn to for help and protection.

You gave your little ones holiday presents. Will you see how near you can make of the year one beautiful heart-holiday for them, and then they will love you so much better, and when comes the time, stand between you and life's storms, no matter what they be.

We know men and women who have cows, horses, sheep, and pigs more cared for than their little children. Perhaps it is because a horse or cow will bring money. But all the money in the world is not such sunshine to the heart as is that earnest love, without which life is but a succession of cross purposes. Children need this love. The father who spends his days in idleness, his nights in dissipation; who lets the foliage of language fall from his lips torn, stained, broken, worm-eaten and full of poison, is weaving thereby a carpet for the young soul he should teach, so full of shame, pain, sorrow, and blight, that no outer dress fashion may dictate can make atonement for.

Kind words are diamonds, pure and of untold value. We know a father who is very rich; he has five children. He buys them presents, and is proud to see them well-dressed and well-behaved. But he never joins them in plays, romps, and games — it is undignified! When " father " speaks, it is like the tolling of a bell. He commands — they obey, as do dogs! He is making *men* of his boys, so he says!

We know another man, with three children. He is not a rich man; only a worker. But he is kind, and full of happy thoughts. He is loved, respected — almost worshipped by his home ones. He laughs with them, romps with them, and helps them to make little toys — teaching his children all the while to *rely on themselves* for something to help interest, amuse, and instruct. He spends his evenings at home. He wears clean clothes — puts his dirty apron and jacket away in the shop, and takes pains to go home with clean hands and face, and a glad look. He reads to his little ones evenings. He tells them stories — incidents of his life and observation — till the little ones think, in all

the country there is not another one so good,
so kind, so loving, and so full of knowledge as
is their father.

His home life is very beautiful and harmonious. He began right, years ago. He never
spends a night or day in dissipation. He lives
for those he loves, and who love him, and is
walking as straight to everlasting happiness as
ever a bullet flew to pierce the centre of a
target!

One day we heard that his children were
better than other children. That they were
better behaved, and always looked so smart,
attractive, and intelligent — when they have
help to develop rather than an existence of un-
certainty between fires and cross-fires. If all
parents were good to their little ones, or half
so careful of them as of their furniture — when
a soul is easier marked than a piece of wood —
the world would be better, and in a short time
all would be as brothers, eager runners in the

race for happiness and honorable reward ; not only here, but beyond the resting-place, and the schools we shall find for parents and children in that land whose opening gate is life's final Saturday Night.

CHAPTER XXI.

ABOUT A BRIGHT-EYED BABY.

THE street cars were crowded to-night as we rode home from down town — from the office and the types, and the presses, and the whir of machinery. The workmen were nearly ready to leave, for the last edition for the day and the week was on the press — the army of newsboys were on the streets with the paper just from the press, gathering their harvest of pennies from the eager buyers. Said a fine-looking gentleman beside us in the car:

"Saturday night again! Are you not glad? I am."

"Yes, we are glad — not so much for ourself, for our work is not finished."

Then the car stopped — a woman with a sweet, clean, loving face came in. She had in her arms a pretty baby, a few months old. The gentleman with whom we had been conversing, gave her his seat, as he was soon to leave the car. She was a woman about twenty-four years of age. Evidently the wife of a workingman.

And the baby. Such a sweet, clean, bright-looking little one! Its tinted cheeks, bright eyes, clean lips and face — its nice little white cap of Berlin wool, with blue ribbons — its little, white cloak, with neat blue trimmings; who could help looking at the little innocent?

So we looked. And smiled — and winked. And with our eyes talked to the little one. And it laughed and jumped, and seemed *so* happy. And we had a nice chat with the baby. And the passengers smiled at its happiness. A few crusty people in the car sat cold, stiff, dignified, "manly!" looking as though it were beneath the dignity of manhood to add to the happiness of innocence, or to lighten a heart even for a moment.

But what of them or their stiffness? They were babies once — so were we all. We talked with the little darling, and it kept laughing in glee. And we talked with its mother.

"Is this your little one, madam?"

"Yes, sir."

"How old is it?"

"Ten months."

"A beautiful child!"

"We think so at home."

"And so bright — sweet, clean, and good-natured."

"You think just as we do."

"Always so good-natured?"

"Yes, sir."

"You and its papa ought to be very happy."

" Oh, we are, sir."

" Does he ever get drunk and abuse you ? "

" My husband abuse me? No, sir. He never was drunk, that I know — he never even spoke a cross word to me — not one that was ugly."

" Nor you to him ? "

" No, sir — I love him too well."

" You must be very happy then. And with such a nice baby."

" We are, sir — we always were."

" What does he do nights and days ? "

" He is a foreman in a piano shop — he works there days, and nights he reads to me — plays with the baby — plays backgammon with me, and rests."

" Well — *God love you.* You, and him, and baby. Tell him another workingman said so. — Good-night."

" Sixteenth street ! "

So said the car-conductor, with a nod to us, and we, too, were home or near there.

And all the evening we have been playing with that little baby. We see it now all over the paper before us.

Perhaps it was not dignified to play with a bundle of innocence on the cars! Well, who cares? Baby and we liked it — and its mother was not displeased, and many an eye looked just as we felt.

"How could we talk to its mother and not know her — without an introduction?"

We knew her! Her face told us who she was — a good wife and mother. Her baby introduced us — a higher power, that of Innocence, introduced us. We meant no wrong, no impertinence. And think you a woman does not know when a man means well — when he is a gentleman? She read us aright. Would to God all people would do so. Then we could do more good.

And so to-night we thought we would write of the baby. God love the little innocent — all the little ones who have good mothers and good fathers. And all who have not good parents to love them, and to care for them. And all the little foundlings and orphans who are without love, and who must walk for years under trees that have neither flowers nor fruit.

We have been thinking of the dear little babies all over the land, and of the little ones who are sick and dying as we write this — of the little pets who have gone before us to their rest, escaping the heat of the day, the torture of heart, the weary struggle and net-work of temptations about us who are growing old!

We wish all the little babies were as clean, as happy, as well cared for as the one we saw to-night. We wish all of them had good mothers and fathers, who never spoke cross words to deaden hearts and love for each other, or to make the little one wonder, as it grows up, why people who love each other so often talk cross, quarrel, scold, and set for the little watcher bad examples. Little pitchers have big ears; young eyes see — and young memories are the best!

And we have been thinking of mothers who care more for dress, gossip, scandal, ease, novel-reading, and street show than for little babies. Of mothers who are in good health, but too fashionable to take care of their own children. Of mothers who are dissipated and filling their blood with poison to give as legacies of disease to other little babies, which to them in time may come if the laws of God and life be observed. Of the women who have nice babies, and love them, O! so dearly, just as we pray their little one may ever love them. Of the poor women who drag their love, their life, their bodies out of shape and into the grave bearing babies only to please a lazy, selfish husband, who devotes his energies to raising children to support him in his declining years, as one would buy a horse to do his work.

And we have been thinking of the poor women who love their babies, but who cannot dress them even decently; who have no loving husbands to *care* for them, and who, with heavy hearts, sigh, and wish, and wonder if their children ever will look nice and be of use in life. And we have been looking back over the life of the mother we talked with on the cars.

— A happy girl. Married to an honest-hearted man. Not a scion of snobbish aristocracy, living on the labor of others, but a young, working man. Joined together by God, in love and devotion. Their lives in unison. And thus they begat a child. No fear, sorrow, remorse, terror, dread, nervousness and doubt of him, his love, devotion, virtue, honesty or ability to care for her and theirs — no cross, cold, unkind, heart-cutting words to affect the unborn as nature molds natures! No petulant, uncaring days of neglect and abuse. And so they lived. And so baby came. And so it is good-natured, bright, happy — and so it will make others — for the line of God-given love loses not by the wayside, but extends from conception to dissolution, and even into the Land of the Leal, as thread left by the shuttle, whose hither and yon weaves the fabric to patterns as we direct! A happy woman! A happy wife! A happy mother. A kind husband. A noble man. A common laborer! One of God's monarchs, who will reign in the hereafter, and help by their deeds here and work there Him who was and is the greatest laborer of all.

A brave, true, home-loving man. He spends not in dissipation. He romps with his baby. He reads to his wife. He enjoys home games. He is not ashamed to love and to be loved. He is fairly worshipped by her who cares for the baby and for him as he cares for them. He dare be a man. He dare save his earnings, his honor — his manhood — his life! God love him, and all such — yes, *God* love all who do not love their home ones — who do not love themselves, but who throw their lives away — their powers to do good forgetting, and who live to no purpose except to labor to enrich the dealers in dissipation, or the slave-holding aristocrat.

And we have been thinking how a woman will and does love such a man — one who loves her, her home, her little ones. How proud she is of him. How strong in his love. How protecting in her love. How sweet her life is to him. And this is life — as God wished and intended we should enjoy — as all would, but for their dissipation and weakness.

Perhaps some of those who read this are too dignified to play with babies! Too proud to unbend — too cowardly to follow their better natures. If so, we pity them. May God give them kinder hearts, but not take from them their babies — their darlings — before comes to them another and a better Saturday Night.

CHAPTER XXII.

THINKING OF THE PAST AND THE FUTURE.

THE pain has passed away. With the week just gone, it rolled silently down the depths of the past, leaving us one Saturday Night nearer the golden future, and the reward we are more than confident it will bring. And now that the week has gone, taken with it the thousand cares it brought, we are glad, and all the more ready for another seven days' battle with life, and those troubles which with singular energy so steadily crowd to fill the path before us. But troubles will come — as we who would conquer must trample them down and press on — and on, and still on. For only those who strive will reach the goal.

And now that the most blessed of the nights named is with us, let us rest. Are you weary? Then sit in your room, or with the one or ones so dear to you, and living every minute in your heart, and think a little to-night.

.   .   .   .

We have been thinking and thinking a full hour.

"And what of?" you may ask. We will tell you. Perhaps you will laugh at us, and say we are not *manly*. But we care not for that. The record of our life here goes before us to Over There, and it matters not, when we go for such reward as may be ours, what any one here may or may not think of us. The record is perfected There before the act be finished Here.

.   .   .   .

We have been down the well of time. Into vapory memory. Walking again the life road

we for years have been stepping over. We
have called up all the childish faces we knew in
the years agone. Have visited the old spots
and haunts where as a boy we rested, rambled,
and built air-castles. We have been in memory, with our school companions — with our
playmates. With the friends of our youth, and
looking over the acts, good, bad and indifferent,
which fill the pages of our past — which have
made so much of the volume which will be finished forever when shall come some Saturday
Night.

We have seen where we made missteps, and
where we stepped by or over thousands of
temptations. We have seen where we would
have done differently here, or there, if it were
ours to walk again the cruel, tortuous, rugged,
dangerous, torturing road, over which so far we
have safely journeyed. We have looked back
at little chances to have done good, which we

neglected from carelessness, and have made good resolves for the future.

And we have looked at the lives of our companions, or many of them. We have followed them as, perhaps, they in thought sometimes follow us. Some of them sleep — no! they do not sleep! Some of them, when came the time, closed their eyes and brought their lives to a *whisper* here, to see and to speak *aloud* Over There. We have walked to-night down the aisles of memory by many a grave and recollection, as one day, perhaps, some one or ones will pass by ours. .

Some of our early companions live — some do not. At least, not here! Some of them went Over the River, loved and happy. Some of them fell by the wayside, and went out with that tide which rolls to restlessness. Some have married, and many have mourned. A few — a very few of all the ones we knew are happy, while many are not. But of them all, *not one* so happy as we are. At least we would not give our happiness for theirs; our *full faith* for their doubts — our earnest work for their hours of play.

Many who were our friends then are our friends now, and God knows they are dear to us. And some there are who a few years since would not speak to a child of poverty, who now do not see fit to remember that once we were too far beneath them in the scale of wealth to be noticed. As if money made the man, or wealth made us noble!

At times we have felt envious. And who of us all have not? But now we envy no person in all the world. Some we know are richer, but we would not give *our* friends for *theirs* — our heart-rest for theirs — our *happiness* for theirs. Some there are who have made fortunes — but hoarded gold rests on the coffin-lid too heavy for the soul to rise perfect to that Power to which it belongs.

We all at times look back and feel envious of the success of others. But when we have done our best, we have done all they have. If we have not, the fault is with us. And while many have done better, how many of our old friends and playmates have done worse? Who of them have been happier and more respected? Are not most of us better off than many, and many who started life with us?

Years ago we were very poor. Money we had none. Friends were not so plenty as now, for we had not by long and honest endeavor won them, or tried to, by so living as to deserve confidence. But we always hoped for the best. We were willing to work, and always willing to wait. And to the one who is willing to wait the morn, the night is always the shortest. Life with us has been a success. More so than to many others. We have health. We have strength. We have a willingness to work. We have a constitution carefully guarded to middle life, unbroken and unweakened by dissipation, other than follows overwork. We can see already good fruits on trees we have planted. By labor we have turned our muscle into support, and intellect to at least reasonable use.

Before us on the desk is a watch marking almost the midnight hour. A little thing of itself, but we earned it. On our finger is a ring bearing Masonic emblems. We earned that also. And the desk on which we write — the pen in our hand — the beautiful pictures on the wall — the piano standing there to give out at times the music which so rests us — the carpets on the floors — the vases, statuettes, and ornaments of the room all about us, are nothing of themselves, but we earned them. They surround us with encouraging presence, telling us to go on. We see by this presence that we have lived to a purpose. That we have beautified our place of labor until people say it is a parlor. We see that we have given employment to artists, artisans, mechanics, and genius. And thus we have helped others in turn to beautify their homes.

So we live, day after day, in the midst of works of our own creation. We might have spent more time idly, but our health would not have been better. We might have spent what we earned in dissipation from the first, but are not these articles of beauty more a source of happiness and of gratification to friends; more a good example and incentive to poor boys and deserving men everywhere, than a form bent, a body ruined, a face marked by dissipation?

As we see what we have accomplished, we feel stronger for further efforts. And all the more so, for a bright face haunts us still. A kind and loving heart bids us rest from labor in its gentle sunshine; kind words come to us, and eyes which talk volumes of God's language, speak to us so often. And so, in all the world is there no peace like the one we have earned.

No friends like ours ; that is, none so good, so true, so kind, so earnest, so confiding. We have something to live for. As all who read this have. What we have done, others may.

Other men can be kind and they will be. Other men can earn beautiful homes, and can make their workshops attractive. And they will. Other men can have money for books, pictures, etc., and enjoy the present — or they can live aimless lives, and sleep in the bitter dregs of a misspent existence.

We would not write this now, but we love the boys and the workingmen of the land, who deserve homes of their own, and hearts of their choosing, and love to protect them. We love the brave, earnest poor boys of our country, and so sit to-night to tell them that by work and a care for their manhood they can be rich and happy. Not that wealth is required to make *us* happy, but to enable us to make *others* so, and thus add to our own.

We love the earnest men of toil who dare be men — who dare strive for usefulness — who dare make their homes attractive, and who dare live for their loved ones. And so, with a heart reaching far out to the little homes of the land, do we love to sit and write, as if we were talking by the hearthstone and fender; to talk socially and in quiet kindness to our friends, and to bid them and their good wives and happy little ones God-speed — to wish for them all a happy life and beautiful home, not only here, but in that glorious Land of the Leal, which all of us are nearer by another Saturday Night.

CHAPTER XXIII.

NOT SO LONELY AFTER ALL!

JUST as our hopes come and go are the weeks lifted into the invisible, as in time all of us who read and who write — who love or who hate — who toil or idle, will be. And how short each of these weeks is as we look back from this to last Saturday Night. And yet the past week has been a long one, for since last we sat by our desk to bid the week "good-by," and watch its fading memories floating Eternal-ward, a loved friend has gone home to await our coming in the beautiful land where all words are kind and all shadows golden.

And so they go. Why can not we who are tired, weary, heart-sore, and overworked go at once, and not wait till the sun goes down and every minute of the day worked out? To-night we feel sad. The air seems filled with strange, plaintive whisperings, as if friends of the invisible were mourning at our tardiness and blaming us for not being with them before our time — before our allotted work be finished. They seem to tell us that loved ones over there are each day coming from beautiful groves and flower-lined walks to the shore of the sea which rolls from time to eternity, but never this way, to see if we are not yet arrived. As our loved ones over there are waiting and looking for all of us who are good, and true, and kind, and loving.

To-night we are all alone — save the golden presence we often feel, and so often see, when with it we wander leagues away, over plain, hill, valley, mountain, and sea — over the

wondrous sea of Death, but ever returning till
we cross it aright, as others over there have
crossed. But the sunshine from over there
rests in our heart continually, and it gives such
light and peace to the mind. We have no
more fear of the kiss of death than of the
cooling ice which is so grateful to fevered lips.

. . . .

Back to our room which in spirit we left an
hour ago. And we have been, O! so many
leagues away. We are lonely. Did you ever
feel as if the very air was thick — as if no one
could penetrate it to be with you? Did you
ever sit and long for the presence of some one
till it seemed as if the soul would fly? Did
you ever sit and think of some loved one till
the heart would be stilled as if pulseless
silence forever, and it seemed that you must
cry out in agony?

To-night we have felt so. It seems as if
there were nothing but duty in the world —

as if there were no end to this wearying labor. O! if some one who is absent could be with us. If some one whose smile is our life — — whose heart is our resting-place — whose lips are so sweet — whose hand is so soft — whose life has so run and woven itself in with ours — whose eyes seem to us like avenues to the Eternal, could be with us as of yore. If we could hear that loved voice — could hold to our heart the one we know beats more for us than for any other person of all God's millions — could sit palm in palm resting — could rest our aching head and wildly-throbbing temples on that bosom where it would be so welcome — could rest, and feel all the while that none were so truly happy as we who would thus add to our love and happiness, how light would be our heart and sweet our rest this dying hour of the week.

All the week have we labored — perhaps having done some little good. We have tried

16

to be good. Last Saturday Night, wearied, overworked, nervous, and disappointed, we forgot ourself just once and uttered a cross word. God knows we have suffered for it. The memory of it comes with its blackness, to chide and cast a gloom over the heart. We should not so speak to-night. We have not so spoken since. And God being our help, we shall no more speak so, for cross words are unmanly, and cut like red-hot blade of steel to the very quick of the soul. There are no cross words spoken Over There; and oft while others sleep we go there to listen, to look upon the face of the one who is our guide and strength.

If we cannot conquer ourselves we cannot conquer death! If we cannot teach our tongues to speak kindly to others, how will others speak kindly to us? And how weak we all are! Who of us can walk alone? And who so brave of heart as the one who is loved, for this is God's armor! How one can toil — can wait — can suffer — can battle on manfully — can struggle as did Jacob with the Angel from Heaven — can endure — can resist temptation — can defy danger and trouble, if there be to protect and encourage, the true, earnest, living love of a kindred heart, all, *all*, ALL your own. If we are but loved, the hours seem like minutes — the labors of the day but pastime — the trials of life but little patches of shade over the sunlit sward. God bless all who love each other — no matter who they be — who they love — mated or unmated, for our mating here is no more our mating over there, except hearts grow together, than the darkness of earth is the sunlight of Heaven. There are no chains over there — no longing for something not to be had — no crushing under the ponderous wheels of mistaken duty, as heathen are crushed under the car which bears simply the idol of their own creation, as their "religion" dictates.

But we shall be with the loved and absent before long. The days will fly quickly, for they shorten as we near the grave! And then we shall rest. Then we shall look deep into those eyes. And sink · like a child to sweetest slumber into the heart we know, for God has told us, beats for no other one on earth. And we shall smooth back the hair from that brow — shall hold to our heart the one that throbs responsive, and *then* will come the glorious sunshine which leads us ever on through the dark and weary hours of those who are lonely.

All there is of life is love. Ambition is but crumbling straw to be burned by time. It dies upon the lips, but enters not the heart to lighten and make truly glorious. All these conquests — these adding of acres — this piling up of wealth for others, is nothing to the growing of that love for others which will carry us

safely over the wondrous sea where those
whose hearts are heavy with lust, passion base
and selfish, desires only for personal gratification, will sink to rise no more.

Then let those love who will — who can — for
thus are we joining hearts for the Eternal, .
where it will not be good for·man to live alone.
And rest those who love — closer bind them
together, counting as lost hours those which
keep united souls apart, as the light is kept
from fruit and flower to wither and fade and
fall before its time !

. . . .

And though we are lonely to-night, sitting
with the dying week, we are not lonely, for a
gentle presence is with us. We shall meet and
be where the heart is, all in good time. And ·
then the eyes will be brighter — the lips
sweeter — the brow smoother and more lovable
— the heart happier — the golden promise
more than realized as eyes talk, and touch of

love thrills with wild, strange, ecstatic emotion.

And we are satisfied with our little loneliness, soon to be over with, as we think of the weary, heart-wrecked, wretched ones, who have no loves to make them happy. Of the poor little children who are orphaned, or whose parents do not love them. Of the lonely wanderers who have no homes, but who are the driftwood — the flotsom on the sea of life — with hearts water-logged and sinking into the bad from lack of buoyant love.

And we are not lonely for all — when soon we shall meet with our loved and absent. These days will soon pass away. These weeks will soon be gone. We shall be the nearer the shore and the starting on our voyage. We are not so lonely as the men who are unloved — who are lost to themselves, to others, to life — to ambition — to love — to happiness from that dissipation they would be happier to walk away from. We are not so lonely as many a man we know of who works, and works, and works, but who has no loving heart to welcome him home — no neat, clean, sweet, loving, true, kind-hearted, caressing, affectionate, soul-cheering loved one to watch and welcome his coming.

We are not so lonely as many a poor woman who was loved, and caressed, and given presents, and led along by promises of love, constancy, and devotion forever, years ago, when the one who is now a cold, selfish, reckless, passion-gratifying husband was her lover. We are not so lonely as many a poor woman who is living in a cold home, with nothing but rags, or labor, or sorrow, or child-bearing, or sickness, or her heart-crushing "duty" to live for, simply because society demands sacrifices God does not! We are not so lonely to-night as many a woman whose loving heart has been wrecked — whose furrow-marked face tells us exactly her grief, as we see where the lines of care are planted — whose soul fairly shows the coming of the husband whose touch is agony, whose kiss is sickening, whose passion is her pain, whose ecstasy is her misery, whose presence her despair, whose word her, law, and whose love is but selfish tyranny! God pity these poor lonely ones — the heart-wrecked mudsills on which society rests its barn-like prison-house of Christian duty — as if it were the duty of a Christian people to torture the soul and crush the heart as heathen do their bodies, or to palsy their affections as heathen do their arms and bodies in doing penance.

And so, thinking of these soul-sorrowing ones the world dares not speak kindly to for fear of offending tyrants, we are not lonely. Very soon we will be with the loved and the absent, and then we will rest, and be loved, as we shall rest, shall love, and be loved beyond the quiet hours of our final Saturday Night.

CHAPTER XXIV.

PUT THEM AWAY.

TICK! Tick! Tick!

How the ticking of the clock, unnoticed at other times, strikes like hammer of iron to the heart as we sit here to-night, in a room yesterday occupied by a living, loving friend! To-night she is at rest in the Golden Land. And we mourn — not so much that she is out of pain and bodily agony, but that no more on earth can we hear her voice — listen to her encouraging words, or look into her eyes that so eloquently mirrored the purity of her soul.

To-morrow, so soon to be here, will be the Sabbath. Day of rest — *Day of sadness!* for a dear, good friend has already in this life won her crown and place with those who have passed on, while we are left to win ours, but with no more of that help which came from her good wishes, pure counsel, and beautiful, unselfish friendship.

No one in the room with us — save the guardian spirits, each with pure, loving thoughts for us to give to others. What is left of her lies in another room. The door is just ajar. All is still — very still in there. We listen and hear the ticking of the clock — nothing more.

Let us see! Twenty years ago we sat, as now, in a room much like this, while a friend, or the temple in which he once dwelt, rested in a room adjoining. We were then as now in the presence of death. Then we were not at rest as now. The wind howled without. We were afraid. There seemed then to come a shadow of terror from the " waiting-room."

Were you ever afraid to be with the dead?

"This was her room. O! Memories! Wherever the eye rests there is something to remind us of the absent one."—*See page* 251.

Did you ever fear to be alone with death? If so, we pity you, if your fear and sufferings were like ours in the years agone, before there came about us a light as came to one long since — as comes to many who are deserving. But to-night we are not afraid. Why should we be? There is nothing there to harm us. Only a lesson — that our home is not here. While we work, she is at rest. While we listen to the ticking of the clock, as Time marks those who have "gone home," she is waiting on the shore for the one whose very heart, soul and life, she won by her purity and kindness, while here to bless him with her love and Heaven-born influence.

Others mourn with us. They sleep in restless beds, to waken in tearful sorrow while we keep watch of the flying hours, each laden with souls going from here to the beautiful Land of the Leal.

This was her room. O! Memories! Wherever the eye rests there is something to remind us of the absent one. There is a little watch-case nearly finished, as she left it until her recovery! There is a book in which she read but three days ago. Here is a little ribbon worn in her hair, which we kiss with tear-wet eyes. She has gone! It is so still here! It is so lonesome for those who are left alone to look at the little articles worn or used by the absent ones. We pity, O! so deeply — those who weep, and watch, and pray — those who are left to wait in the storms of life, while the loved one waits on the distant sunny shore.

There is a slipper once worn by her — a glove — a thimble once worn upon the finger now so cold and lifeless. In that little desk are letters and scraps, and kind words from others to her. In that little jewel-box is a ring, and a few other articles more precious than wealth, for they were hers. All about the room we see her still!

O, Father in Heaven — why is she not here, with her kind words — her pure love — her eyes so full of beautiful language? Why cannot those who love *go home together* when so true to each other they walk the paths of life here? When we must part some day, if only for a time, why do we not live better, purer, truer, and more loving for each other than for self? We can not find our way or live our life alone so well as with a heart united.

Then, good angel; merciful Death! come for those who are left to mourn, and bear us to them, from pain to ease — from tears to smiles — from grief to joy — from separation to uniting. Then will you be a welcome — welcome — welcome visitor, and we reach forth to call you to us, as a babe reaches for the hands that are to bear it to the bosom of love.

On the walls are pictures she arranged. She made everything so homelike. All about are evidences of her work and care, for good women are so much more thoughtful than most men. Here and there are evidences that she lived and loved. Garments she wore till it seems now as if a portion of her life were left therein, so much did she individualize everything about her.

See there ! A necklace worn about her neck since months and months ago, when joy filled the heart of the one who placed it there as she said —

"I thank you *so much* for it!" We heard her say it — and she knew the one who gave it to her was happy, because she was. What makes the tears come so? *She has gone —* but she is here !

Put them carefully away! These sacred reminders of past happiness. Let no rough hand disturb them. Put them all away, wet with tears, and when tired of this battle of life, look at them, think of the absent one, thank God that there is a beautiful Land of the Leal, where those who truly loved on earth will meet, and live, and rest, and walk and work delightfully together; where thought is the implement and minds of men the field of labor for ages and ages to come.

So, welcome Death. Welcome the Dawn!

For what is death but life? The opening of a door through which loved ones go to better and brighter lands — to wait for our coming. Then we will put away these things we have looked at and wept over, and put away that terrible idea of a bigoted, ignorant past, that Death is dreadful, for *it is not*, only to those who are educated to fealty to man more than to God, and to be content with ideas more than principles, without which there could be no God, no creation, no progression — no Eternity — no rest beyond the final Saturday Night.

CHAPTER XXV.

HOW SOME POOR PEOPLE ARE VERY RICH.

HIS Saturday Night we are very tired, and weary, and nervous, and lonesome; for the work of the week sat with unusual severity upon brain and body. Once, when younger than now, we never counted the days nor the weeks. But now we do. Each day is one less! Each night we are nearer the wonderful morning! Each Saturday night we are so much nearer the separation, for a time, from that earthly love and beacon guidance which every true man has hung in his heart to love, adore, and confide in.

And each day counts for or against us. As

we near the end of the race we try to make up for lost time, but too often our strength has been spent till we stumble and fall, never to rise till the race be lost to us and won by another.

We have tried all the week to be good, and kind, but it was harder work than usual. We had so much work to do. Little things have bothered and worried us; at best we are only human. Those we called friends have lied to us, and forgotten promises. But we have not broken faith with them. So we dare look them in the face, as they dare not do by us. How good it is that we are not to answer for the sins or misdeeds of others! . .

And yet we are happy to-night. There are others more weary than we are, and with no one to love them — there are those who have no golden-tinted hope of love on earth or rest Over There. There are those for whom loving eyes are not looking — some loving heart not beating — some life running so close, even, and beautiful in with theirs, from here to the very face of a smiling God, whose greatest reward is rest and happiness. Not so with us — so we are happy.

And we are glad to-night to think that thousands and tens of thousands often multiplied, all over the land, who have toiled and been perplexed all the week as we have, can rest and sleep this Saturday Night, if we must work.

.   .   .   .

To-night, as we were coming up the steps leading to our private rooms, opposite the cooling fountain in the little park before our windows, a policeman handed us a piece of paper, on which was written, with a lead pencil : —

SATURDAY AFTERNOON.

Will you please call at No. 12 — Tenth street, room seventeen, third floor back, sometime this evening to see two persons who cannot see you? If asking too much, don't come, for we are poor people.

Room 17 — third floor, back. Half-past nine at night.

"Come in!"

Now, good friends, and especially little boys who wish to be useful men, and little girls who wish to be good women, we will tell you of our visit.

We went to a tenement house. Twenty-one families live in that crowded five-story brick house. Poor families they are all, too. Somebody said, "Come in." So we entered, to find an old man and an old woman there. The man told us he was fifty-seven. The woman said she was but fifty-three. And these old people were both blind. No wonder they could not see us! They lived in a room twenty by eighteen feet. Two windows looking out into a small yard. Two windows under which two cats were squalling — "just as they always do when we want it still," said the old lady.

In one corner of the room was a bed. In another corner was a sort of lounge, on which a person could sleep. Two chairs were in the room, and a little half-round table up by the wall. And a few clothes hanging on the wall.

The old man sat by a window smoking a pipe. The old lady sat by the other window smoking another pipe. Out in the street children were romping, though the night was hot.

"Good evening, friends. This is room 17, and you sent a note to-day by a man who gave it to a policeman to hand to us when he saw us."

"This is room 17. Are you Mr. Pomeroy?"

"Yes."

"We hope you will pardon us, sir — but John said you would come if we wanted you to, so I thought you would come, and we sent for you. It was so good of you to come. This will be a new day for us old folks to count from."

"Thanks, good woman. Who is John — and what can we do for you?"

"Oh, nothing, sir, only we wanted to hear your voice so we could know just what kind of a man you are. John is our boarder. He is night-watch in a store down town, and goes on at nine and stays till six, sir."

"And you old people are blind?"

"Yes, we are blind, but la! that's nothin' when you once get used to it, but it did hurt a good deal at first."

"How long have you been blind?"

"Nineteen years, and Betsey has been blind twenty-four years, as she was long afore I married her."

"Then you never saw her?"

"No; but I know just how she looks, for a blind man can see, if he hain't got eyes!"

"What do you do for a living?"

"I sell matches on the sidewalk down Broadway, and Betsey sells 'em up town, and we keep a boarder besides."

"Does he pay for his board?"

"What? old John pay for his board? Indeed he does!"

"How much?"

"He pays all. We all of us gets the stuff to eat, and old John cooks it for us night and morning. But Betsey and I pay the rent. Old John cooks and sweeps, and Sunday he does the washing, except what we do. And he reads us the papers, and we know all that is going on. He reads to us a little at night before supper, and after — then he goes to watch, and we talk over what he has read."

"Do you and Betsey love each other?'

"Yes — better than all the world. It was a good day when old John brought us together, and we love him for it."

"What do you do when one or the other is sick?"

"Oh, we get along — take care of each other. But we don't get sick as other folks do, for we don't eat such rich food, and have better health."

"And you are happy here, both of you?"

"Indeed we are. Old John's eyes do for all of us."

"Are you a Mason?"

"I am — but I don't go to Lodge since I am blind."

"And you wanted us to call here? What for?"

"Oh, we wanted you to come. Old John *said* you would come, but I didn't hardly believe it. I wish we had something to offer you."

"You have — a kind welcome. And nothing on earth is more God-given or beautiful in its memories."

"Well, you are welcome. But I want you to tell how you write such chapters each Saturday Night? And they don't sound like other reading. Somebody must help you?"

"Somebody does."

"Who is it — a man or a woman? It must be a woman — and yet it can't be!"

"It is neither — but a beautiful thought — a golden-faced presence, that comes to us with a troop of followers from the Land of the Leal — a beautiful spirit who makes us happy — who keeps us from danger, who comes when we call, and tells us that we shall, surely rest Over There, if we strive to do right here, and live to our line of light and belief in duty."

"Yes, yes! I know now! Just as I thought — as I knew — for some one comes when I call — when we call. And we are very happy. We shall have eyes Over There — but eyes are nothing if one don't use them."

"Quite right. And you are happy here?"

"Yes; with the help of old John, for which we give him a home. We have but few friends, but they are good ones. And we don't see much to annoy us or make us envious. We don't bother about the fashions. And then we don't care what others say of us — we live for each other, and are always happy."

"But you are blind!"

"Yes — but that is nothing. It hurt me at first, but I learned to accept a fact as such, and when one has learned that lesson he has won a victory."

. . . .

For an hour we sat and talked thus with our blind friends. And it was a beautiful lesson we learned. That people can be happy, no matter if blind and poor. That living, not for the world, but for those who love us, brings to the heart the greatest reward. And above all — that one who learns *to accept a fact as such* has won a victory.

And to-night, as we think how much we

have to be thankful for — how much more blessed we are, as the world counts, than this poor old couple, we feel light of heart, rested, and strong. In their home is no unkindness — no cross words — no selfish indifference, but a deep, earnest love for each other — a desire to make the most of circumstances, confident that after this struggle for existence will come a beautiful rest with those who love us and are beloved, beyond the weary Saturday Night.

CHAPTER XXVI.

THE LOVED AND THE ABSENT.

ANOTHER drop from the bucket of time into the vapory amethyst — another week lost here to be pinned as a star Up There to light the Heaven. All these weeks — each of these Saturday Nights — are but stars, each one adding to the glory of the future, as one by one they are lifted home. His record of Time, to last through eternity. Some stars are brighter than others, as some weeks went Home laden with less sin, evil, wrong, selfishness, and heart-blackness than others.

To-night we are all alone in our room, but

not in thought.   We have silent company.
Without, there is the hum, the noise, the
bustle of city life and restless humanity.   The
air is keen and cold as man's charity.   Within
all is light, comfort, and attraction.   The fire
burns in the grate — the black coal turning to
white ashes as our acts are purified by the fire
of trouble, sorrow, struggling and agony of
the heart wrestling for the prize it craves.

The carpet on the floor — the rug on which
our kitten sleeps, seem warm and earnest in
their colors, like the life of an earnest man,
whose heart-work carpets the floor of life, so
that others may walk with less noise, and rest
thereon more comfortably.

The chandelier overhead throws its mellow-
tinted light all about, just as kind words and
honest eyes light and warm the heart.   The
pictures on the walls — the keepsakes everywhere to be seen seem sociable, as if each
wanted to tell us the history of the ones who

have thus kindly remembered us. Who would not be happy thus surrounded? All these beautiful things won by honest labor. Better these evidences of striving, than a life of dissipation, with good to none!

But something is lacking to-night. We all lack something! The loved and the absent. By wondrous power we can go to them, if they cannot come to us. And we will go. . . .

Here is written evidence — a little scrap of paper on which was written "Once upon a time," and we will go on a visit to our darling. You cannot go with us. The smiles and the tears — the hopes, joys, griefs, sorrows, and inner life of those we will soon visit are not for you to know.

.   .   .   .

Home again!

We saw her — but she did not see us — yet she wakened with a start, and tried to listen, to look light into the darkness as we bent over her couch. We went because it was lonesome staying alone when the heart is away! We had light — light from the window, burning in Heaven, placed there and watched by one who for years has thrown that deep, clear, wondrous light full across, and far along our pathway to guide us safely where others often fall. We went as thousands who read this chapter wish they could go to their loved and absent ones, but cannot see the way because they have not thrown the shade of bigotry from across the soul.

As thousands of the good, the true, the earnest-hearted, the fearless, loving, caring, working ones wish they could go in a body to visit their loved and absent ones.

We saw her.

We talked with her as she slept. We wiped a tear from her eyes, and she wakened with a trembling start — we passed a hand over her face never so lightly, and again she slept.

Did she know we were there? Ask her! She knew somebody was there, though the darkness was like a pall to her vision.

And she slept. We held her hand in ours. We held her to our heart. We saw the trouble go for the time from her spirit. Then we lifted her carefully in our arms and kissed her closed eyelids, that when she awakened our image might never pass from her. And she did not awaken. Thus light and pure is the kiss of true heart-love given in person or spirit. Then we kissed her hands a dozen times, that the touch of none other might be as ours — then we whispered that one dearest of all words, *Darling*, in her ear, and her face responded to the joy of her heart thus given to bask in the sunshine of love. Then we left kisses on her lips — sentinels to guard the heart none other may win, and noiselessly departed as we came.

Do you ever think of your loved and absent

ones? Do you hunger for that heart-rest which gives joy? Are you never lonesome when the loved ones are absent? The loved one — the one best loved of all? Do you not often wish that one were near you at home, or elsewhere, to enjoy with you the beautiful of life — the kiss of love — the touch so filled with God's electricity? Are there not times when the hours drag — when you so long to be with the absent?

Or are you so lost, so crushed, so wrapped in selfishness as to be content to live half a life without the bliss which follows making others happy? No — no — none of our readers are thus lost — thus storm-tossed on the clouds, their present unloving and their future but guess-work! Are you at times weary, heart-sick, needing rest to soul, to brain, to thought? Would you visit the loved and the absent — giving life and light to both hearts?

You can if you will! If you live aright.

Not like trembling, cringing, terror-stricken, uneducated, bigoted slaves to that narrow-minded education you too often call religion. Would you have a beautiful home? Then, good brother, strive to make it so, for you are the master if you so will it.

There is something glorious in being a man. In feeling in your heart that you are true, earnest, honest, and of use, if not to others, at least to yourself. It is the germ of power to control yourself — to keep your heart warm, your words from roughness, especially to the loved ones — your brain cool when battling with life — your mind and body well and whole, with vigorous manhood, gentle touch, and love's electricity, when comes the hour for home joys, and communion with the loved.

It is glorious to be able to sustain yourself — to know you can walk where danger threatens — can run where others grope — can live where others but stay — can be loved and

18

pitied, and cared for as God's sunshine and moist dew cares for the tender plant — can be loved, and held to the heart all the home hours, while many are but *endured* by the home ones your dissipation has made sick at heart and desert-lifed forever.

Those who are unloving here, will be unloved over there. Those who fool themselves away here will not be counted over there, more than the worm-eaten bud which drops to the gutter in June will be a flower in July!

Would you have others to love you? Then be kind, liberal, forgiving, charitable, pleasant-faced, and considerate of the feelings of others. Would you have others look to your coming with anxious delight, glad when with you — lonely when away? Then be a man — simply yourself just as God intended. Do not be forced by education, dissipation, or self-ishness, to grow out of yourself into the morbidness of lust, thirst, love for power, or desire for dissipation till all the glorious, the man-like, the good, the godlike be frozen out. All this is with yourself. For as you will — as you elect for yourself — as you have the honor to be — as you have the will to dare, so in exact proportion will you have the power to accomplish. And thus can we all become better, stronger, more loving and more with those loved, but often absent when comes the morn of the morrow, or the resting hours of Saturday Night.